SPECIAL MESSAGE TO READERS

THE ULVERSCROFT FOUNDATION
(registered UK charity number 264873)
was established in 1972 to provide funds for research, diagnosis and treatment of eye diseases. Examples of major projects funded by the Ulverscroft Foundation are:

- The Children's Eye Unit at Moorfields Eye Hospital, London
- The Ulverscroft Children's Eye Unit at Great Ormond Street Hospital for Sick Children
- Funding research into eye diseases and treatment at the Department of Ophthalmology, University of Leicester
- The Ulverscroft Vision Research Group, Institute of Child Health
- Twin operating theatres at the Western Ophthalmic Hospital, London
- The Chair of Ophthalmology at the Royal Australian College of Ophthalmologists

You can help further the work of the Foundation by making a donation or leaving a legacy. Every contribution is gratefully received. If you would like to help support the Foundation or require further information, please contact:

THE ULVERSCROFT FOUNDATION
The Green, Bradgate Road, Anstey
Leicester LE7 7FU, England
Tel: (0116) 236 4325
website: www.ulverscroft-foundation.org.uk

THE BARONET'S PRIZE

Yorkshire, 1816. Horace Richards, heir to the Kinsley Hall Estate, dies in France after losing everything to Sir Christian Leigh-Bolton. When Horace's sister Eleanor is thrown out of her home by his widow, she seeks refuge with Mrs. Jennings, her mother's retired companion.

With Mrs. Jennings, Eleanor creates a plan to rescue her future — but when the handsome Sir Christian returns to England to claim his prize, will the attraction she feels for him betray their subterfuge and turn her world upside down once more?

VALERIE HOLMES

THE BARONET'S PRIZE

Complete and Unabridged

LINFORD
Leicester

First published in Great Britain in 2021

First Linford Edition
published 2025
by arrangement with
the author

A catalogue record for this book is available from the British Library.

ISBN 978–1–4448–5459–6

Published by
Ulverscroft Limited
Anstey, Leicestershire

Printed and bound by CPI Group (UK) Ltd., Croydon, CR0 4YY

This book is printed on acid-free paper

1

June 7th, 1816, Kinsley Hall

'Sit down, please . . . I have grievous news!' Jemima swept into the small breakfast room seizing Eleanor's attention away from the two set places on the mahogany table. Each morning Eleanor waited patiently for the woman before breaking her own fast. Her sister-in-law's brusque manner along with the unusually sombre mourning attire alarmed her.

'Whatever is it, Jemima?' Eleanor hesitated but the woman opposite pointed to the chair pulled slightly away from the table in readiness for her, so hesitantly Eleanor sat down.

'Horace . . . is no more!' Jemima declared dramatically and gripped the back of her own chair.

'What?' Eleanor's mind spun. Possibilities whirled around, not least was the question, what was Jemima up to now? Always one for drama, and for demeaning Eleanor by constantly reminding her that she was her husband's spinster sister, and as such a burden to them to be borne for the family's sake. 'You mean Horace is lost in action?' Eleanor asked her stomach clenched as Jemima gracefully descended into the chair opposite as a bemused servant set about serving them breakfast.

Eleanor had lost all appetite, which was just as well as Jemima dismissed the servant and returned her focus to Eleanor.

'No, I mean, I am a widow at not yet thirty years of age . . . and my poor baby, Quentin is without a father. A man who died a hero for his country . . .' She sniffed delicately into a handkerchief.

Eleanor fought back tears. The lovable, foolish brother she recalled from her childhood was dead. 'When? How? There has not been a letter or news this last week.' She paused as another option occurred to her. 'Did you have a bad dream, Jemima?' She wondered about the state of her sister-in-law's mind. Had she finally crossed over from being fashionably dramatic, loving her agues and tantrums, to fanciful notions bordering on madness?

'No there has not. I have shielded you from this dire news this last month since Horace's solicitor visited me.' Jemima declared.

Eleanor gripped the edge of the chair's embroidered seat, defying her instinct to stand and deliver a verbal onslaught at the selfishness of the woman opposite.

'You have known for over four weeks, and you did not share with me that my brother had perished! Did you not think I had right to know too?' Eleanor's voice rose but she was greeted by what was obviously a prepared speech; Jemima had this conversation planned and as Eleanor's grief hit her hard it was all she could do to keep up with events as they unfurled, and unfurling they were — like her life.

‘You simple girl! Do you not realise how much of a shock this is to me? Not only have I lost the man who promised to love me forever, but worse still, through no fault of his own, he has been outwitted and the estate will be taken over by a stranger . . .’

Eleanor had bristled at being referred to as a ‘simple girl’, but indignation was replaced by disbelief and horror at this new revelation.

‘What? How so? This is my home!’ Eleanor said defiantly. ‘It cannot be!’

‘No — that is not the case. Kinsley Hall should belong to me for Quentin’s future but alas, I must fall on the charity of my dear cousin Edward who resides in Kent. He has no heir and is some years into his maturity. Edward has kindly agreed to accept us into his household and make Quentin his heir.’

Eleanor’s mind reeled with unanswered questions.

‘How can Horace have ‘lost’ the estate to a stranger? It has been in our family for four generations.’ Anger and grief mingled along with the awareness of how Horace had been drawn to the gaming tables in his adult years.

'The solicitor explained it all to me and assured me that it is the truth. Horace died a hero, and his reward has been to lose his home. Tragic as it is — that is the situation!' Jemima swallowed and sniffed delicately.

'Did he gamble it away? Tell me honestly!' Surely Horace had not returned to the gaming tables like the Horace of old? 'Did he lose it to pay a gambling debt?'

'How dare you besmirch his memory?' Jemima pointed her finger at Eleanor who did not flinch. 'He died so others might live.'

'Who is this stranger that now apparently owns my home? Where is he? When is he coming?' Eleanor fired the thoughts out as they struck her.

Jemima vaguely waved her hand to dismiss Eleanor's questions. 'That is of no import. You do not need to concern yourself with such notions.'

Eleanor's thoughts were racing. If Horace had lost her home, then he was a dead fool and no hero. Jemima had disliked Kinsley with its cool North Yorkshire winds, forests, and wild moorland atop the slopes of the hill sides dotted with the sheep. The locals depended upon them for their living. The woman had longed to return to her family in the south. Tunbridge Wells was both fashionable and busy enough for her to poach another father for Quentin. Eleanor shook her head. Defeated she may be for now, but she would seek answers and plan her own future. She needed space and time in which to do this. 'How soon do I have to be ready for this move to Kent — it is so far away?' Eleanor stood up and shook her head willing the tears to stay behind closed lids.

'You will not be travelling with us. I am afraid you cannot burden my cousin Edward like you have your brother. You will stay in Northallerton with your aunt.' Jemima helped herself to some toast and blackcurrant preserve. Her appetite apparently restored.

‘You expect me to ‘burden’ my aunt? Is this arranged also?’ Eleanor asked, desperately sipped her coffee. She felt light-headed and needed to stay alert. Shocked to the core she may be. At least if she was to stay with Aunt Amelia, then she could possibly have time to recover some of her possessions from the Hall. Perhaps her aunt might raise objection to whatever Jemima’s plans were for the family home.

‘You will have to visit her. I have written a letter of explanation which she should receive before I leave.’ Jemima ate delicately.

‘When will that be?’ Eleanor asked.

‘The day after tomorrow. Baxter will take us there in the coach and four. It will be an arduous journey.’ She shook her head regretfully, but it was Eleanor who felt the despair.

‘Two days! You give me grievous news indeed and only two days to prepare myself for losing my home. I need to pack my things, there are letters to write.

I should have mourning clothes. Have you no heart, Jemima? Do you really hate me that much?' Eleanor asked. 'And what about the staff? You have dismissed people already, now I know why. It was nothing to do with their behaviour or cost, was it?'

Jemima slowly lowered her cup before meeting Eleanor's gaze. 'Eleanor, I have no time or energy to consider you at all, let alone the staff. I have a son to provide for and a cousin who is more of a gentleman than Horace could ever have been in this backwater. So, please find your maid, whilst you still have one and have her pack a bag that you can carry. You will need to leave tomorrow. I could not abide lingering, emotional goodbyes.'

Eleanor stepped back, dropped her napkin on the floor and walked out — numb and speechless. But the anger that was building within could erupt like a volcano. Eleanor would seek justice for her brother — her home and whoever the wastrel was who had taken Horace's inheritance — somehow Eleanor would make them dread that they ever set foot inside Kinsley Hall.

2

June 9th, 1816, Northallerton

Eleanor approached the grand terraced house with a heavy bag that matched the onerous feeling in her heart. She tried to brush the dust off her boots before she lifted the polished door knocker and then waited to be given entry and announced. Breathing deeply, she glanced back down the High Street — stay in control, she told herself. She could feel the panic that had been bubbling away inside her rising. Jemima had placed her in a humiliating and desperate situation.

She had walked since being dropped off the dray which was travelling on to Thirsk. The ride had been warm under the full sun. Mrs. Minerva Jennings, who used to be her mother's companion and friend had told her straight, 'You're on a fool's errand!' Yet, Eleanor could not believe that. Who else to turn to but family? Her bloodline had run through her deceased uncle — yet family was family! Aunt Amelia would welcome her into the lovely spacious home, wouldn't she? Four Christmastides ago, when Eleanor's circumstances had been so vastly different, they had been given a warm reception, but had only corresponded by letter since, it had been too long, ever since Horace had married Jemima.

With a creak and a groan, the highly polished black door opened revealing the familiar chequered tiled floor of the immaculate entrance hall inside.

'My card,' Eleanor said, offering it to the young maid who was staring blankly at her. 'I wish to see my aunt.' The servant's expression showed surprise at the absence of a chaperone or carriage. She stared at the card. 'It is most urgent that I see her . . .' Eleanor explained. The maid showed Eleanor inside. She paused, marvelling at the contrast of the floor against the pale lemon of the plastered walls. Memories of flickering candles, bright green and red holly and mistletoe garlands festooning the hallway, filled Eleanor's mind — happy thoughts. The distinctive smell of citrus fruits and spices flooded back to fill her now dulled senses, sparking life for the first time in what seemed like an age. Eleanor smiled, relieved to be here, remembering fondly the welcoming warming glass of mulled wine as the guests had entered this sheltered privileged world.

'Wait here, miss — I'll see if the mistress is receiving,' she said.

Eleanor dropped her bag by her feet and watched the girl place her card on a small silver tray that had been left on the hallway table for this purpose, and then skip easily up the sweeping carpeted stairs. Grand Grecian columns lined the side of this magnificent entrance. Kinsley Hall was just as grand, originating from an earlier period in history. Unlike this bright interior the oak that lined its walls had darkened over the years; still magnificent, but a stark contrast to this new building. Eleanor decided she would soon adjust to it. The weight of the burden began to lift from her shoulders, and she absorbed a moment of peace. Her life would not be the same, but here at least it could continue as she was accustomed. Perhaps her aunt could help her find a suitable husband, despite Horace's foolishness. Oh, when would she be free to mourn his death? She was too angry with him at present for losing Kinsley.

The door upstairs was opened as her aunt's voice resonated off the hard walls. 'I am not in, Ida. Tell her that I am not in!'

Eleanor's gloved hand flew to her mouth to stop a sob of disbelief escaping as the words echoed and drifted clearly down to the hallway.

'Inform her I have gone away with her cousin Harriet, and we do not expect to return before the Season. We shall not take in penniless strays!' The door was closed. The words had clearly been meant to carry to her ears so that she would be in no doubt they were meant.

The confused maid ran back down the stairs to deliver the brusque message, but Miss Eleanor Richards — the penniless waif — had heard the dismissal loud and clear and had duly turned around, leaving of her own accord before she was humiliated further by the delivery of her aunt's shameful rebuff.

Outside in the street, Eleanor glanced back and saw the curtain in the upstairs morning room flicker. Her only aunt had made her stance on Eleanor's unfortunate position clear. She was a social outcast! She swallowed back the tears before they cascaded down her pale cheeks. She could be homeless and destitute as far as that woman was concerned! How that hurt! Eleanor had not realised she could feel any more desperate than she already did.

Eleanor tilted her head back, whilst looking out from under her bonnet's brim and walked off towards All Saints church. The bustling town of Northallerton had always been a favourite place of hers and her brother's.

With only a few pounds between her and destitution, along with her own meagre possessions — those she could carry — she was a gentle lady fallen on diminished circumstances. Should she be a governess? A companion? She shivered even though the day was warm. That was a soulless, lonely road to poverty in old age. Jemima had been given Eleanor's mother's jewels by Horace, except for a ruby necklace that he had not known about. That was not all, though. There were other small gifts, some quite valuable ones, that her mother had told her to keep safe should Eleanor ever need funds after her own passing. These Eleanor had carefully hidden away within a box hidden in the attic. It had been hard advice, but mother had obviously realised what Jemima's arrival could mean for Eleanor's future. Jemima had used Horace! They were married in France, Jemima was the young widow of his fallen captain, who had found herself in an 'awkward' situation. Horace had stepped in and honourably helped her, or so the woman claimed. That was the past; how Eleanor accessed her other maternal gifts now was a mystery to solve. She must somehow stay nearby and wait her opportunity.

Eleanor's feet already ached. She must return to the only friend she apparently had left who might help her, Minerva Jennings. Walking down a narrow side street she stopped by the back of an inn. Not an ideal place for a young lady, but she was so tired! It had been a wild hope that Samuel was still there. Fortune, it appeared, was at least providing her with some good for a change. 'It's Samuel Higgs, isn't it?' she asked, as if she did not know who the son of the dairy farm on the estate was. By sheer chance earlier, she had seen him turn his wagon around behind the inn but had dashed down a snicket to avoid embarrassment. Now her pleasure was hard to contain as she saw him readying his empty wagon to return to the estate. How quickly things changed, she thought, as she watched the recognition dawn across his face grasping her bag to her.

'Aye, miss,' he said. The horse was hitched and ready.

'I wondered if you would do me a kindness,' Eleanor asked, and tried not to sound as desperate as she felt, despite being alone with a heavy bag in a side street late in the day.

'If it's in me power to do so, miss, then aye, of course.' He tilted his head on the side, curious. She tried to subdue an urge to smile because momentarily he reminded her of her father's old cocker spaniel from her happy childhood. What a lovely time that had been in her life.

'I wondered if . . . well you are returning home are you not?' She tried not to lose her confidence as the light would fade soon and she had no wish to be found alone out on the streets.

'Are you wanting a lift, miss?' he said quietly to her. 'Is that it?'

'If you would not mind, Samuel.' She let out the breath she had been holding and nodded back. He instantly jumped down and helped her up to the front seat of the wagon. He touched his flat cap as a mark of respect, even though this was all highly irregular.

Samuel lifted her bag into the back of the wagon with little effort.

'It's no bother, miss. You'll be more comfortable, and cleaner sat up here with me, miss.' Then he added, 'We all feel your loss and, well, if it's Minnie's you be heading to, I reckon I can pass by her door. Her cottage is quite hidden, miss, so no one need know. It's deep in them old woods down the old mill track.' He winked at her, kindly, without mocking.

Eleanor could not help but wonder how many of her father's long serving estate workers knew the truth of her situation and of Horace's loss — of life and inheritance.

'Splendid! Thank you, Samuel,' she said, hoping if anyone who knew her from her normal round of acquaintances saw her from their fine carriages leaving on a wagon with a farm worker, they would not realise who she was. Then she frowned as one undeniable thought struck her — what if they did? Carriages were hardly lining up to whisk her away to offer her sanctuary!

'You worry none, miss. Good will win out.' Samuel climbed up next to her; at least he seemed genuinely pleased to have her company.

How could he possibly understand? Yet she blinked because what did she know or understand about his daily life, the wars, or the impact of losing the only provider in the household on foreign soil. His father had perished five years previously and Samuel had since taken over the farm. Perhaps they had more in common now than Eleanor realised. Words failed her as she contemplated the humble door that she had to knock on next. Humility, Ellie, she silently remonstrated. She had to be grateful for small mercies and kindly folk like Minerva, or Minnie as her mother fondly called her, and Samuel.

Eleanor was helped down outside the gate to Minnie's cottage. Hatred was a strong word, but what Jemima had done to her made her wish the woman far away, well she had gone. Yet that too was unkind for did she not have a lovely innocent child dependent upon her? Oh, tears welled; she would never see Quentin's little face again. Eleanor's blinkered father had never seen the flaws in Horace's nature: her soft-hearted and possibly stupid brother's desire for pleasure over hard graft. Horace was bought a commission in the 51st Regiment. He had the business acumen of a laundry maid, but not their work ethic. Eleanor would survive and come back in force and Jemima would eat humble pie at Eleanor's table. It would not be revenge, but she would see justice done.

First, though, she had to survive!

3

'No luck, my dear?' Minnie asked before ushering her inside the cottage taking her bonnet and pelisse. Candles flickered and an oil lamp glowed from a small adjacent room. It was tiny to Eleanor compared to the spacious high-ceilinged rooms of Kinsley Hall.

Eleanor shook her head. She did not want the woman to gloat even if she had every right to.

'Told you, lass, eh! Your type of folk run a mile from scandal and, well, young Horace died in . . . 'uncertain' circumstances and lost his inheritance into the bargain.' She coughed. 'Now, let's head through to me cosy kitchen.'

Unless Samuel talked to more than the cows on his farm, Eleanor's present whereabouts would remain unknown. Minnie's short, rotund, apron-clad figure glanced back at the closed door, as if the birds and trees were trying to listen in.

Eleanor could not bear it anymore. She had loved Horace and could never see what attracted him to the venomous witch he married. What were the 'uncertain' circumstances Minnie referred to? Jemima had told her that he died a hero, yet no details were given as to how. That did not explain how the ownership of Kinsley Hall had been transferred to a total stranger. She had never even had the opportunity to read the letter that the solicitor delivered personally to Jemima. Eleanor had seen the legal representative arrive but, unknowing as to what his business was, she had passed the time of day politely with him until her sister-in-law was free. He never even hinted that he brought such dire news.

'There is no scandal in a man dying too soon, Minnie!' Eleanor said.

'Well, Napoleon's finished, and your brother must have been one of the last to go there and to fall, unlucky blighter. Pardon me, but when luck was shared out, they missed his cup, lass.' She coughed. 'Also, to gamble away the estate! He was no hero. Anyways, come on, Ellie, can't have you standing here; sit by my fire.'

Eleanor thought 'Touché!' as the woman had addressed her in kind. Only Horace had called her Ellie since her mama died five summers previously.

She hesitated, wondering what she would do now if this kindly woman also turned against her; patience and tolerance would need to be her watchwords until she could remove herself to a more respectable living.

Eleanor had never worked a day in her life, and it showed. Why should she have? As the lady of the house, until her brother married it was not expected. She had been tended by their servants. What could she do anyway, other than teach the things she already knew to children? How would she obtain a governess's position without a reference or an introduction? The thought of it made her pale: living as a shadow figure between the family and staff — a life of isolation, except for her wards. It did not appeal to her at all.

'Ellie, have a tot of brandy, while I rustle up some batter pudding and ham from my larder. Don't look around at my home like that; it doesn't do to look a gift horse in the mouth — so to speak. You look like you're lost, but this cottage is plenty big enough for two. The Henderson's had eight under its roof and they thought it a fine place to live. Crikey, whole families live in one room cottages on the estate, so this is like a palace.' She chuckled but her eyes showed that she was clearly making a point.

Eleanor stared along the narrow hallway — the low cruck frame roof and roughly plastered walls.

'Look, Ellie, you have been spared from total ruin and starvation so be brave. If you reject my kitchen's offerings and my spare bed for a place to kip, then the streets are a far lonelier and colder alternative; especially for a fine lady like you. Your pa would have been rocked to the core if he had known that your own family had gone and left you like this — all alone.'

‘That sort of thought is not going to help me now, is it?’ Eleanor snapped out her words, but her eyes were watering, and she swallowed hard. She was so hungry and tired; ashamedly the tears were ready to flow.

‘Yes, well, I’ll forgive that remark because you’re damned right! Now, none of that snivelling here — no blubbering!’ Minnie stepped back and let Eleanor pass her by. Three rooms led off the hallway: a front parlour, a bedroom, and the kitchen. ‘Your ma was a fighter, and I loved that woman dearly. Now you dry those eyes of yours and after you’ve fed and rested, we shall set them on a clear course, where things will look much better.’ She raised both eyebrows, but Eleanor passed by her without word whilst she breathed in her tears and swallowed deep.

‘I’m sorry, Mrs. Jennings, I did not mean to be disingenuous.’ She wiped her eyes with the back of her gloved hand.

‘Good, whatever that is, I’m sure you didn’t mean it, cos you are a good lass and I'll help you, but you are going to have to come down and meet me in my life as is, as I cannot climb that ladder to reach the one you had. So, are you staying?'

Eleanor nodded and forced a smile to her lips. No answer was needed, but she cleared her throat.

'I shall be honoured to stay here. Perhaps I can pay you a small rent or . . .' Eleanor had no idea what else she could offer. She was not prepared to sell her mother's rubies if she could avoid it. For one thing, if she did too soon, and word managed to reach Jemima, Eleanor wondered if she could accuse her of being a thief. How would she be able to bargain a fair price on something that to her was priceless? How would she know what they were worth or how to sell them even if she wished to — which she did not. Eleanor would survive until time and distance was placed between her and the sister-in-law she had begun to hate; a strong emotion that Eleanor had never thought she was capable of.

She must retrieve her belongings. How though? That would be a question she would answer once she had eaten and rested.

'Oh no, lass, you'll not pay me a farthing. You are not to be my mistress or my lodger. You will stay here as a friend or my companion, but you help when asked and I will show you how to live happily again — or at least contentedly and that is more than many ever manage.' Minnie bobbed her head to stress her words whilst her cloth bonnet flopped against her wiry greying hair.

'How to live?' Eleanor looked mystified. What was the woman asking her to agree to do? She wanted to trust Minnie, but she felt like she could be in the jaws of a trap. To give her word of obedience and then renege on it was unthinkable. She was a lady who mixed in the limited society of the county — yet had been excluded from it because of the circumstances surrounding Horace's death. The world loved a gambler when they were successful but disowned one who lost so badly as to forego their inheritance and home. Eleanor knew so little of Minnie's life.

'Yes, survive, and learn to live a quite different wholesome life, find a respectable way through the mire, because, my dear Eleanor, you have been left knee deep in one that would not look out of place in a pigsty. So come and have a natter with Minnie, and a brandy with some food on my kitchen table and see how the other 'alf live. For them folks on the street out there are slowly starving, love. There is no work for returnees from the wars. So, look on my humble fare with a kindly and grateful eye.'

Eleanor sat on the rickety chair by the small range and sipped brandy from an old, chipped porcelain cup that she recognised from her mother's set back from when she was a child.

Minnie nestled into a comfy chair after placing a plate with a large slice of Yorkshire Pudding and ham on top of the range as the gravy warmed in a pan with leftover turnip from the woman's meal from the day before. 'It'll be ready soon; you sip that and drink it down good, lass. You've been walking around Northallerton most the day, haven't you, trying to pluck up courage to come back to Minnie's door?' The woman shook her head. 'You should have come here first and stayed. I don't bear grudges against them that did me no wrong.' She took a sip of her own drink and slapped her lips together. 'John provides some good stuff, you know.' She shook her head and added quietly, 'Or perhaps you don't.'

Eleanor agreed, she didn't know. The brandy dulled her senses, coupled with the comfort of the heat from the range, and nestling in the old chair made her feel strangely relaxed, sleepy if she was not so hungry. She could hardly deny Minnie's blunt observations; she had been wronged by Eleanor's family.

The crooked table, small range and two worn out chairs were taking up most of the space, Eleanor realised Minnie had not hesitated to share the little she had in the world with her. Next to

Eleanor was the only cupboard, housing the larder.

A sensation of feeling both lost and found at the same time swept through her. It was strangely comforting — or was that the effect of the brandy? Fortunately, at least she had been left a small income from the estate that Jemima and Horace could not touch. If only her mother had left Eleanor something independently, her own cottage, but she had trusted Horace with that duty at least - to care for his sister.

'Ah, that's better. It's amazing how a tot of brandy can clear a person's vision. You shall be as my own lost daughter — aye — that's it! If I'd been blessed with one, that is.' She nodded.

With the drink and the appetising smell of the warming food on the range Eleanor fought the urge to sleep; her stupor was broken when the harsh dismissal of her aunt's words resounded in her head. Society's door had closed, and Eleanor was on the wrong side of it. Yet, here instead of being desolate as she ate, her happier childhood memories flooded back. Yes, she would do well here. She would learn to live!

'Thank you, Minnie.'

'Aye, lass, thank you for I am sorely in need of some good company and a steady hand that can sew. Feel free to butter me up, lass,' Minnie winked and chuckled.

Eleanor felt no menace in the woman, but this time smiled back somewhat tentatively.

4

Sir Christian Leigh-Bolton was forced to arrive at Kinsley Hall in the dead of night. An oil lamp was flickering in a downstairs window. He had the key; it was heavy enough to anchor a man-of-war, Christian had bemoaned, when presented with it along with the house deeds in the offices of Bellingham and Crouch, of High Street, Northallerton.

'Good God!' he exclaimed as he threw open the large oak doors and stared into the dark depth of the hallway, placing his tall hat on the stand, along with the key. He did not see why he should have to slam the lion headed brass door knocker down hard to announce his arrival.

The ancient-panelled walls were just visible in the poor light making the place appear gloomy like his mood. He preferred a lighter ambiance. A broad, wooden staircase disappeared into the shadows at one side of the entrance hall.

He continued straight into the library, having studied the estate's plans Christian knew where rooms were located. A sad looking fire dwindled in the hearth; it was losing the will to survive. The lamp was also succumbing to the night. Loosening his greatcoat Christian rubbed his hands together. Someone would have to see to his horse, it also needed caring for. Where was the damned housekeeper? She had been notified that he, the new owner was coming!

'Sorry, sir.' A flustered Mrs. Hitchins scurried past him without stopping, making for the fire, and grabbing the iron to poke and rekindle it.

'Sorry, sir,' she repeated, 'I nodded off in the chair. You must have been exceedingly long in the saddle,' she said, her wits apparently still half in sleep. 'I was sent word that you would be delayed as your uncle had taken ill,' she said, standing straight again. Stifling a yawn, she added, 'But didn't think you'd arrive this late . . .'

'Well, he died.' Even to Christian his

words sounded as cold as this insufferably long night had been. 'Please wake the cook from her bed and tell her that I need something hot to eat and soon before I join my uncle! Then get the stable hand to see to my horse. It has brought me a long way.' His words were snapped out like orders, he was not in the infantry anymore, but such habits were hard to break, especially when you were cold, hungry and bone tired.

If the damnable coach had not lost a wheel between Ferrybridge and Wetherby he would have at least arrived in some warmth. The woman hesitated, looking near to tears. She stood before him in her night robe, shawl, slippers, and cap. She had not stayed up; of course, she wouldn't, he had not been expected to arrive in the dead of night. Christian's arrival as he opened the door made enough noise to awaken the dead. What a first impression to make upon his staff!

'Just ask her for a plate of food, cold if it must be and a glass of her best brandy.'

He tried to look pleasant now that his face was not so frozen and was regaining some of its normal animation.

'I cannot, Captain. You see there is no cook.' The woman took a step backwards when he spun around; his attention had been on the fire where he was warming his hands and enjoying feeling the blood return to his cheeks.

'You jest, surely!' he said, but could plainly see by her wan pallor in the limited light from the lamp she was carrying, that she did not.

'I was waiting word, Captain . . . er . . . Sir Leigh-B . . .'

'Sir Christian, will do . . .'

'Sir Christian, I was waiting for your instructions. But there was no word and so I could not stop people leaving.' She swallowed.

'I am supposed to be taking over the Hall, the estate in its entirety, fishing rights, tenants and staff.' He stood straight suspecting that all was not as he expected it to be.

'Well, the Hall is in good order. The

tenants are anxiously waiting for you to tell them what is happening under your ownership, the estate manager left, sir, when the Master's wife fired him. That was the day before she too left. The staff is much reduced. I know nothing of the fishing rights . . .' her voice trailed off.

Christian detected a trace of sarcasm until he raised one dark eyebrow, even if it was hardly the woman's fault. He had been duped, it appeared, by the luckless Horace. The dishonourable cad, Horace, had traded him the Kinsley estate in its entirety yet had ordered his soon to be widow to diminish it before she too left.

The circumstances of the transfer of Kinsley Hall were due to Lieutenant Horace Richard's ruinous gambling. The transfer furnished a vast debt owed to Christian, created by Horace's hedonistic lifestyle. Ultimately, the man had ruined his health prematurely — he had been a rank coward. That aside, the estate was supposed to have been fully staffed, but like a fool Christian had not ascertained by how many servants.

‘Most of the staff were stood down, by instruction of the Master, Sir Christian. Everyone presumed it was at your request . . .’ Her lips clenched into a thin line.

‘So how many staff am I blessed with?’ He realised this woman was holding back pent-up anger and would love to vent it at him but dare not — rightly so for he had done nothing underhand or wrong.

The woman shifted uneasily. ‘Counting myself, four. The gamekeeper, John Squires, who lives on the estate and has been trying to keep the place together, and then there are two maids, Annie and Florrie, one upper, one kitchen cum laundry.’ She cleared her throat. ‘Together we’ve kept the place going for the past month, sir, since the master died.’

‘Can you trace any of the original staff?’ he asked.

‘Possibly — some will have taken new positions . . . in Thirsk, or on the manor houses hereabouts . . . as I have also done, Sir Christian.' She tipped her head up slightly, bracing herself for his response.

'What!' he snapped at her, and she flinched taking a step backward.

'Yes, sir, I leave in two weeks. I cannot survive without any payment for my services, even if your intentions were to make up the arrears. Besides, the lady of the house gave me an excellent reference and recommended a physician's household in York. She was lovely, so beautiful, and it was so wrong what happened to her . . . Oh, poor Miss Eleanor . . .' her hand shot up covering her mouth.

'Then the lady should not have married a drunken, gambling buffoon!' he snapped the words out and buttoned up his coat again; he would have to see to the horse himself.

'Not 'that lady' . . .'

'No matter! I have heard quite enough for one night. Bring the food . . . as soon as possible.' He attempted to soften his request but was dammed if he was going to ask her.

She walked away briskly before Christian could call her back.

Once his ex-sergeant Bill Raynor arrived with the mended coach, he would send the man back to Wetherby with the horse he had hired. His mood instantly mellowed as it would be good to have Bill back; there was work to do here, even in the dark he could see that. If the household was so diminished, then he needed his loyal friend watching his back and keeping an ear to the ground. It would have been naïve to expect his arrival to be welcomed by all the staff — but he had expected some to be there.

With gargantuan effort he strode away from the warmth of the fireside, making his way through to the kitchens to cut through to the stable yard, expecting to pass Mrs. Hitchins. Once Annie, the young maid, stopped screaming as he mistakenly burst into her room behind the wall that housed the kitchen's main range, Christian managed to get her to realise he was the new master of the Hall and not an intruder. This must be the warmest room in the house he thought.

'Calm down, girl, or one of us will have a fit, and I don't think it will be me. I need food,' he said as calmly as he could as she clung to her shawl as if he were going to rip it away and ravage her.

Mrs. Hitchins entered, somewhat flustered, but she was quick to bustle him out and then she and the girl prepared a mug of some hot chocolate, with eggs, ham, and warmed bread whilst Christian saw to the horse.

By the time he was chilled to the bone once more, he returned to the kitchen where his supper had been left on the table. The girl had retreated to her room, door shut firmly, the housekeeper nowhere to be seen again. He had no wish to find out whether the girl's door was locked or not. It was food he wanted not to scare a young kitchen maid out of her wits.

Christian ate, drank, and fell asleep slumped over the table, his plate pushed to the side. When he awoke with a stiff neck and back, he straightened up. Dawn was near breaking, so he made his way up to the master bedroom at the centre of the upper landing and fell onto the bed. Sleep came to him easily.

He only stirred when he heard the wheels of a coach churning up the gravel on the long drive below his window.

'Ah! Bill, my trusted friend, now we can begin!' Christian was instantly awake like any good soldier who had stood watch in the night. Pulling on his waistcoat and jacket over the shirt he had slept in, he flicked his hair from his collar, he had meant to get that cut into a more fashionable style but he was strangely attached to its length. He descended the attractive, polished oak stairs two at a time and was soon standing calmly in the hall. Christian had to admit, in daylight the place took on a much more welcoming ambience. The morning light made the oak panelling appear warm and the furnishings were homely. Around the walls were the typical decorations of a rural house with a fine carving of a Yorkshire rose set between two portraits which Christian guessed may well have been from the previous generation of owners.

The door was pushed open, and Bill stood beaming before him.

'Not a bad shack is it, sir?' he said, nodding to the walls around him, then added, 'You look like sh . . . Morning, ma'am . . .' Bill shone a friendly smile at Mrs. Hitchins, who now fully and immaculately dressed had appeared from the dining room.

'Good morning,' she replied, and Christian could have sworn her face flushed as she regarded Bill's bristly face.

'Your breakfast will be served shortly, sir,' she said to Christian. 'Should I have Annie rustle up something for your . . . man?' Her voice trailed off.

Christian withheld his urge to grin reading the annoyance in Bill's eyes, despite his impassive expression. 'His man' was enormously proud to have served with Christian but had been a serving soldier, a sergeant, and now had no rank but Christian thought 'friend' suited his position better.

'Yes, Mrs. Hitchins, as he has to return with the horse to Wetherby, once he has eaten and has seen to the coach.' With his back to Mrs. Hitchins, who quickly left them alone, Christian grinned at Bill and walked to the doorway to greet him properly.

'I could've returned to me brother in London you know; I didn't have to come all the way up here to no man's land to be slighted by a harridan.'

Bill's gruff voice was low, but Christian knew that the man's brother was an alcoholic and lived in the Isle of Dogs, so that would be the last place Bill, a very moderate drinker by choice, would take refuge.

'I suspect she is harmless. Anyway, she is not staying. Bill, when you've sorted the horse, I need you to find out where the other servants are — we need them back. Chat to the girl, Annie, in the kitchen. She has been left to be maid of all in a place this size, with only one upstairs to help. Be gentle with her, she nearly had heart failure when I burst in last night. There's a gamekeeper been running the estate in the void — when you return, find out what he is like. Also, what he's been stealing or doing whilst he has had free range to act as the lord of the manor. Lest he's a saint and as straight as an arrow, then make sure he has no intention of leaving!' Christian whispered his orders to the man who raised quizzical eyebrows in return to the last comment.

'Yes, sir.' He stepped away.

'Bill,' Christian said. 'Good to have you here!'

The man did not turn back but chuckled. 'Aye, well, sir, like you said, where the hell else would I be going?'

5

Christian ate a hearty breakfast to set him up for a good ride around the estate. Basic in content, but freshly cooked and certainly a lot better than military fare. Bill would have been greatly offended by the idea as he thought himself to be a better cook than he actually was. However, Christian knew that his resourceful sergeant had put many a half decent meal on his plate when supplies were short in camp. His men had not been so fortunate.

'Mrs. Hitchins!' Christian shouted as he left the dining room. If that woman smiled, he thought, her face might crack like a limestone pavement. She reminded him of a strict governess he had once been blessed with. He had had several such in his younger days, all handy with a cane and Christian had despised them all. Now one sobering realisation had haunted him; he may have caused them hardship. How would a boy have known that, for a single woman of good family to be dismissed from a governess's position could lead to them becoming destitute, who would employ them without a good character reference?

'Yes, Sir Christian,' Mrs. Hitchins broke his moment of reflection and appeared from the morning room like an apparition of doom, with her heavy cotton dress, hair tied in a severe, pulled-back slightly greying bun. Although, she had a pleasant face when relaxed. A chain with keys hanging from it hung off a black leather belt reminding him of reading about ancient Saxon lady's holding the keys to the great hall, or perhaps more befittingly the demeanour of a modern asylum nurse — no, that was too harsh, she was not hard or cruel enough for that. With her hands holding each other at waist height she stood posed calmly, in front of him. Christian may have arrived at an odd hour of the morning, it may have been inconsiderate and his mood boorish, but he was not about to apologise to a house servant because his arrangements had gone awry.

'Ah, Mrs. Hitchins, there you are. Do you know where I can find a good cook who either lives nearby or would be prepared to leave the city for a decent living, with immediate effect?' First things first, he mused. 'And, of course, where I can find a replacement for you?' he added and saw her disapproval of the order of his priorities.

'There is an agency in Northallerton, but they will take time to make a suitable selection — but then good staff are in high demand, especially housekeepers . . . and cooks.' Her nose seemed to tilt upwards. 'However, if you want a woman who would make an excellent housekeeper and who is also a more than passable cook, rather than a fancy one who you could hire in if needed for soirees and balls, then there is a lady who lives on the estate who may help you out. She used to be a companion for the elder mistress of the Hall, prior to Master Horace's possession of it. She also covered for the then cook when she was too busy elsewhere. Her name is Mrs. Minerva Jennings, she lives at Briar Cottage; it was bequeathed her until the day she . . . until she no longer needs it, sir.' She sniffed.

'Until she's dead, you mean?' Christian regretted his direct response as soon as the words hit the woman's ashen face. God, he had been a soldier far too long! She clearly knew this Jennings woman well enough, regarded her highly, and, as a seemingly sensitive soul who could not bear to hear the harsh realities of life spoken out loud, she was offended by his manner again.

'Yes! That is precisely what I meant.' Her words snapped, but the eyes moistened, so he tempered his reply.

'Tell me where this Briar Cottage is, and I will pay her a visit.' He watched her eyes shift a little, she had to answer him, but there was unwillingness there at the same time. Why?

'Well . . . Sir, or I could send her word . . .'

'That will not be necessary.'

'Very well. I thought a man of your position, though, would not venture to . . .'

'I shall take the burden of thinking for me from you. Where does she live?' She glared back at him. Good, Christian thought, he could not abide tears but dislike he knew how to deal with.

'Well, if you follow the path from the rear door of the Hall down through the walled garden, then venture out by the east gate passing the dogwoods, you will see that opposite there is an old lane that goes into the ancient woodland. Briar Cottage is a twenty-minute walk along it, set back-aways. You can't miss it as her herb garden is well tended and that beautiful rose border is divine. Her lavender hedge is something to savour when in full bloom; excellent to use for a bad sleeper too.' The woman's words lifted with some admiration.

'Thank you,' he said, thinking if he needed a gardener perhaps this amazing Mrs. Jennings would be able to advise him on where to find one of them also, that was if she was too busy being the cook and housekeeper to help him sort out this mess. She appeared to be invaluable.

'She may not wish to return, though.' The statement was stark, but Mrs. Hitchins did not embellish it further.

'Why ever should she not? If I make her a more than generous offer, I am sure she will see the sense of it. No one is going to try and revoke her rights to the cottage. Is there another reason? Was she dismissed from service under a dark cloud? I should know if there is stain on her character,' he asked, sensing this woman was deciding whether to risk passing on some titbit of gossip to her temporary master.

'She was abruptly dismissed when her mistress died. It was not done in a kindly way, after fifteen years of service to the family. Master Horace and his wife were not . . . they had her removed along with her things to the cottage on the same day. Mrs. Jennings was very hurt by the insensitivity of her dismissal.' She sniffed again.

'Do you have a cold?' he watched Mrs. Hitchins brace herself.

'Indeed not!'

'Good! You make this claim, yet this Jennings woman was bequeathed a cottage for life — is that not amazing generosity in recognition of her loyal service?' he asked. There was something he was not understanding in this situation.

'Her mistress thought highly of her and made sure she would have somewhere to go should she be no longer needed to care for her.' Mrs. Hitchins did not sniff but swallowed this time to control her emotions.

'Speak plainly, please. Is she of good character? Was there any reason why she should have been 'removed' so quickly?' he persisted.

'Mrs. Jennings is a woman second to none. She is kind, gifted and an excellent companion. There is no stain on her character, sir. Master Horace, however, had not known about the arrangement for her living and it upset him and his wife greatly. They could not upturn it, although they sought legal advice on the matter, as the dowager owned the cottage and the acreage that it stood on.'

'Good. Well then, she would seem to be a suitable person to approach at the moment. Please make enquiries about your replacement. Now I require you to write a list of the staff we need to get this place running properly again. I would also like to see the household accounts for the last six months and the inventories of what the Hall has in its stores and a list of repairs that you are aware of that need doing in order of their urgency.' Her eyes bore into him, but he did not change his stern expression as he waited for her comment.

Her lips tightened. 'I was just going for some air, before I started my day . . . again, sir.'

'Well, you can do that later. Today, I need you to provide me with information that was missing when I acquired the Hall. I can tell it has been neglected.

Now would be a good time to begin it, straight away in fact! I take it you have breakfasted. If not feel free to help yourself to what is left, but I want the task completed today.'

Christian left. He did not give her the chance to walk away from him again.

He would not give the woman time to warn this paragon of virtue, Mrs. Jennings, who resided in her home beyond the dogwood trees, of his arrival, or of his proposition of a return to his employ. Instead, he would take the air and catch Jennings unaware of his intentions.

He was a good judge of character; Horace had been a prize fool, for Christian could plainly see that this estate had great possibilities and the man had lost it on the turn of a card before losing his wits and finally his life. Christian aimed to make this venture work and to stay there, providing livelihoods for the tenants and possibly some returning soldiers. He was done with war and losers. His future here was a new beginning.

6

Eleanor awoke feeling rested, even though her narrow bed was built into a wall cupboard with a cotton filled mattress, just wide enough for her to lay straight in. It was passably comfortable and snug, providing a warm cocoon, walking on cold flagstones had been such a shock to her. The wooden floors, rugs and warm fires of her erstwhile home had not prepared her for the draughts that permeated this small cottage.

The quilted cover she recognised from her old nurse's room in the Hall. A grown man would have never fitted into the bed, but for Eleanor it was a welcome, safe space in which to lose herself; to forget her troubles and feel cosseted. One thing she could not abide was to shut the doors tight and feel trapped inside.

Sitting up, she stretched out in her shift, swung her legs over the side and slipped her boots on as she stood. Once her bed roll was neatly stored, Eleanor took her day dress off the hook inside the door, then retrieved her brush from her bag and closed the bed back up — how strange it was to sleep in a cupboard! Yet it appealed to her childish imagination — a secret space, a hidey hole. Eleanor and Horace had played in a tree house when they were carefree children. How long ago those days seemed now. She smiled as sadness swept through her because Horace as a child had been fun and she had enjoyed his company, but once sent away to boarding school he had changed. Pompous Horace returned and grew more remote, turning into a braggart and then a gambler. Next his love of drink took over, dulling his wits about the time he married Lady Jemima Tuxton. Eleanor blamed her more than the war for her brother's early demise. The woman's ambition knew no boundaries and now she had even taken off with the Kinsley coach.

Slow snoring emulated from the small four poster bed, which Eleanor also recognised as the old nurse's one. The rhythmic sounds told her that her host had not yet woken, so she carried her things through to the kitchen where the stove gave out some little warmth. It was the quickest she had ever dressed in her life and unaided; usually a maid set the fire for her before she awoke so she never had to dress in the chill morning air and her own maid would lay out her clothes, bring her warm water and help her dress.

Deciding that if this was to be her new temporary home she may as well find out where things were. Eleanor peeked into the larder and decided to help herself to the food within. Minnie kept an orderly cupboard. That was reassuring as she had no wish to find out she had mistaken rat poison for a condiment.

Eleanor removed a large bread bap and found a serrated knife and board so that she could cut a piece, which turned out to be more of a wedge, but it made her smile with satisfaction that she had done it herself.

She ate the buttered bread and honeyed ham, washed down with a small glass of warmed milk. She had found a jug in the cold-store cupboard at the back of the kitchen. How strange this feeling was, though, of not waiting on food being presented to her; it was one of exploration into another world where she made all the choices amongst the limited fare, rather than be presented with what the housekeeper had agreed with Jemima should be eaten. It may be a novelty that would wear thin, but at that moment there was something strangely appealing about making things for herself; she felt liberated.

Eleanor opened the shutters of the cottage's living room letting the light flood inside. Then her eyes focused on the well and she burst out of the cottage and ran to the path to where she retrieved the bucket and fetched up a pail of water. Who would have thought that doing these things was such fun?

Soon she had returned to the warmth of the kitchen range and the kettle had heated her water through. She had to return for a second pail of water which oddly seemed heavier than the first. Maids, Eleanor reflected, must be strong and hardy to do this regularly. Eleanor washed quickly before dipping her brush into a bowl of water. She bent over double, running it through her long, dark chestnut hair with careful and slow strokes so as not to cotter or put new tangle in it. A smile came to her face as she enjoyed the feel as it flew freely behind her back when she flicked it loose over her shoulders. The colour contrasted beautifully against the lemon floral print of her day dress.

A sharp knock on the cottage door broke her moment of peace. Without thinking she walked and opened it, deciding it must be Samuel returning with some dairy from the farm as he knew she was there, but instead she was faced with a tall gentleman who, looking as surprised to be greeted by her as she was to see him, removed his hat to reveal a head of thick, shoulder-length, raven hair. He hesitated before speaking then said two quite simple words, showing his obvious disbelief as he uttered them.

'Mrs. Jennings?' he asked, incredulously.

'Yes, I mean, no . . . I am not she, but this is her abode.' Eleanor was suddenly aware that her hair was loose, cascading over her shoulders and that it was not even properly dry. She was standing before this stranger in a humble cottage dressed in a fine day dress.

'Who should I say is calling, sir?' she asked and saw a slight smile appear on his face.

'Who is calling?' he repeated, apparently lost in thought or maybe, she wondered, if he was a little simple.

'Perhaps you could leave your card, sir . . .' she added and saw a glint of humour in his eyes as he laughed at her. Of course, he would not expect to leave a calling card here . . .

'Is Mrs. Jennings in?' He was holding

his hat casually in his fingers. She did not care for his tone. It was as if he had had enough of bothering with her nonsense and was dismissing her.

'Who would like to know?' Eleanor could be equally direct, she thought.

'You are?' he queried, ignoring her request and smirked when she folded her arms in defiance. The man was arrogance personified!

'Ellie?' Mrs. Jennings bustled up the corridor quickly behind her.

She must have heard the knocking and thrown on her dress and wrapped a shawl around her shoulders quickly, hiding her hair under a bonnet.

Before Ellie could answer, she was pulled back and the formidable form of Mrs. Jennings blocked the doorway. 'I am Mrs. Jennings, sir, so what business is it you have with me?'

Eleanor took a step back, but watched this handsome, over-confident man address her protector directly.

'Sir Christian Leigh-Bolton of Kinsley Hall. I am the new owner and I have it on good authority that you are a gifted cook and housekeeper, so I would therefore like to speak to you about a position, if you are at all interested. I would rather not do this on the doorstep, but I need both positions to be filled with immediate effect and have heard that you are more than able to do both or either . . . Although a cook would be my top priority,' he added, taking a breath, and smiled charmingly at her, raising his head slightly as Eleanor's expression reacted to the shock on seeing the man who had somehow taken her home from her brother.

'Well then, you had best come in. This is all a bit unexpected. You need to give me a few moments to collect myself and then we'll discuss your proposition.' She turned around and winked at Eleanor. 'Now, lass, go set yourself to task in the kitchen and we'll sort something out for the gentleman to eat . . .' She all but pushed Eleanor along the small hallway before turning and insisting that Christian sit in her small parlour a while whilst they gathered their wits.

'We'll not be long. You can read the Good Book or admire the view of my garden — not that it is as grand as yours and then we can have a chat, sir . . . as in . . . a 'Sir' you say?' she asked, just to clarify things.

'Yes, as in a 'Sir', I am a baronet,' he explained and seated himself awkwardly on a chair.

'Well then, I better get my best china out!' she said and laughed.

Eleanor was re-boiling the kettle, but she stood with arms folded and waited to face Minnie. The man was no gentleman. He was a thief or an opportunist. Eleanor's emotions ran high. She felt anger and betrayal, she was waiting to reveal her feelings at this stranger. Had he caused Horace's death?

'That man has stolen my home! Minnie, you let him come in here!' She dropped her fisted hands to her side, turning away and staring at the small range as if the heat of her temper would make the water boil more quickly.

‘Calm yourself, Ellie. This could well work to your favour. It was Master Horace who lost the Hall.’ Minnie sat Eleanor down on a stool and handed her a brush. Make yourself respectable and come back in here. Don’t you go fronting him, ‘cos Minnie has an idea that will get you back in your home and to a place where you can sort out them things you never got chance to do. Girl you have to be quiet and humble. Douse the fire in your eyes and the edge from your tongue. He can help you, but not if you go showing that temper!’

‘How?’

‘Do as I say and follow my lead. His type won’t stay around a place like Kinsley long, he’ll miss his clubs, and that will work to your advantage. Now run along.’

Reluctantly Eleanor did as she was bid but her heart wanted to go into the small front room and tell the man who stole her home what a vulgar rat he was. But this was Minnie’s home, and she would respect the woman’s advice, for now.

7

'Well now.' Minnie propped her parlour door open with her body whilst she let Eleanor pass her.

Eleanor carefully brought the tray in sideways so as not to knock the edge and risk spilling the tea on the white, embroidered tray cloth that covered the old wooden stained surface nicely. She could not help noticing it had the monogram of her mother's initials on it but seeing as Minnie was her close friend and companion, she could hardly object to the woman making use of it. She knew that 'Sir' was watching her keenly. Whatever Minnie's plan, they had not got off to the best of starts; she tried so hard not to glare at him.

'Place the tray down on the table, Ellie.' Minnie smiled and straightened her posture genteelly as she oversaw its safe deliverance.

Minnie then followed her into the room.

Eleanor's hair was neatly pinned up and she looked more like her normal well-presented self. 'Sir' moved his booted leg so that she could place the tray carefully and squarely down on the small table.

'Lovely, I'll pour. Come, Ellie, and sit on the window seat whilst Sir . . .'

'Sir Christian Leigh-Bolton is my title, Mrs. Jennings,' Christian repeated but his eyes were fixed upon Eleanor rather than Minnie.

Eleanor tried not to laugh at what had been referred to as the window seat as it was no more than a plank of wood atop a stone sill.

'Well, Sir Leigh . . .'

'Sir Christian, will do, thank you,' he said.

'Well, Sir Christian, you want me to go back to the Hall as a housekeeper or a cook, is that correct?' She folded her arms under her bosom after she had carefully poured out their drinks.

'As a cook would be preferable, but if you are concerned about the financial reward, as my situation is desperate, I am content to be generous.' He smiled; his eyes were now meeting Minnie's gaze.

'Very well, but I am only one person and, although very adept, you need two.' Her words, astute and direct as always, surprised Eleanor as she was speaking to a gentleman, but then Minnie had her own cottage, it was her home that she loved dearly, and it was he who needed Minnie's skills. How quickly the tables turned in this new world that Eleanor was having revealed to her.

'Yes, that is absolutely true. You understand the situation well enough. Mrs. Hitchins has sought a position elsewhere, so I am slightly bereft of staff and local knowledge at the moment. I was hoping you might know where the Hall's previous staff fled to.' He tilted his head slightly and looked to Eleanor who was following the conversation keenly. Yet, she managed to withhold comment until the last statement had been made.

'They did not flee; they were dismissed without warning when the Hall was . . .'

‘Yes, Ellie, I am sure that Sir Christian is concerned with resolving his own problem now rather than dealing with the torrent that flowed under the bridge when Master Horace left . . . transferred ownership to him.’ Minnie cast Eleanor a warning glance.

He raised his hand in a gesture to silence Minnie, which Eleanor found quite amusing. As Minnie’s eyes bored into the side of his head, he addressed Eleanor directly.

‘So, you say that the last owner left his Hall and staff to fend for themselves? I understood he had a wife, a son, and a full complement of staff here. The wife and son were to travel to relatives in Kent, but the Hall would be staffed and kept in good order.’ He looked from one to the other.

‘Was that all you knew of the people who lived in the Hall — no mention of any other?’ Minnie asked as casually as she could do without raising a query from him.

Eleanor was astounded that she had

not been mentioned amongst the list of goods and chattels even. She saw Minnie's frantic, silent warnings to bide her tongue whilst Sir Christian's focus was upon her and decided to do just that.

'That is what I understood, Miss. Was there more?' he asked. His eyebrows rose.

'Well, you'll be missing a coach as it went with the wife and son to Kent.' Minnie changed the direction of the conversation quickly.

'That will be returned in time or compensated.' His expression told them he meant every word.

If Minnie worked in the Hall, then Eleanor might very well be able to gain complete access and that would mean her things, those that were rightly hers, could be regained discreetly.

'I have no idea how the Hall was sold on to a stranger, sir, that was not my business, but there were many people who had to suddenly find positions elsewhere and these are hard times. Many of the local manor houses have a full complement of staff already.' Minnie took his attention back to the matter in hand. 'The poor men who returned from war are suffering still.'

'Yes, as someone who has served, I am well aware of the plight of many of my men who came back whole or broken only to be further dispirited without work.' He cleared his throat as if he had strayed from his intended course slightly. 'Well then, if you two could help spread the word that we are restaffing, I will interview and re-employ anyone whom I see fit to do an honest day's work.'

'We will do just that, sir, but if I may suggest one immediate solution: you could do a lot worse than take on Ellie as your housekeeper, at least for the time being. She knows the Hall well and I would be happy to do some cooking for you as long as I can live in my cottage undisturbed — you do know that I'm entitled, don't you?' she added.

'Yes, I do, but that is not why I am here. I have no intention of trying to take your home from you!'

'You'd have a job trying,' Minnie said, in a moment where her guard and sense slipped.

'Mrs. Jennings, I have laid siege to enemy villages, forts and towns. Believe me if I wanted you gone it would be easy to achieve. The well could have an unfortunate accident, a spillage of some detritus with no witness to testify, then where would you get your water from? The river rights are mine. The paths you must tread to leave your cottage are all on estate land. The goods you barter are grown here, but I could stop my workers trading my goods. You see how an evil landowner could make you leave without venturing to court. But please be assured, I am not an evil man. Only occasionally would I ask you to stay at the Hall, or in bad weather when leaving it would be ill advised.'

Eleanor stilled; these words were not meant as threats — were they? If he was not evil, he obviously knew how to be so.

'Do not look so aghast, ladies. I have no wish to do any of these things, but please let us understand each other; this should be a mutually beneficial agreement.'

Eleanor stared at Minnie in disbelief.

'I see you are a plain talking gentleman. Very well, I can also be direct. As you say, I have rights, but they are still under your goodwill so let us not cross words further. I will help you re-staff the Hall and you take this young lady on as your housekeeper.'

'I . . .'

'Now, Ellie, there is no need to pour out further gratitude. I am sure that 'Sir' realises you and I are doing him a favour when here we are settled with you like my own daughter. Of course, you know the Hall well having lived there with me for so many years.' Minnie cut across a stunned Eleanor and directed her further comments to 'Sir' driving a hard bargain, but as Eleanor followed their discussion, with no hope of intervening, it became apparent that her earning power had just increased from zero to a moderately generous wage. A good third more than Mrs. Hitchins had been given by Horace and Jemima, and so Eleanor smiled.

She would have the keys to the whole house and yet be invisible. Not seen or heard unless summoned and she would be able to secrete her belongings away in the cottage over a few months and then... what? Go and stay with a distant friend in Bath, she thought of more friends locally. She would write to them to ask if she could visit and if they would help her situation. Surely Lord and Lady Blockwood would be kindly in their view; after all, she and their daughter Heather had been friends since they met in Harrogate two summers since. Her uncle was a bishop, so their Christian kindness should surely lift her up again in society. She would still be living at the Hall, wouldn't she?

'Does something displease you about the arrangement, Ellie?' Sir Christian asked.

'Heavens no! How could it? The lass is speechless. Mind she will have to be called Mrs. . . . can't have a housekeeper called 'Ellie', can we? I mean you don't want to damage reputations. Yours or hers.'

'Mrs. what?' he asked, smiling at her. He obviously was not concerned about damaging his own reputation.

Eleanor looked at Minnie who had faltered. 'Mrs. Avery,' she supplied and smiled, for that was Eleanor's grandmother's name, and her mother had always loved the woman dearly. Lady Eleanor Gloria Avery was Eleanor's namesake. It was a family name, passed down, but not one he would ever trace as it was on the maternal line. So, she told a lie and set her course. It may become unravelled as soon as a member of her previous staff referred to her as Miss Eleanor with their customary polite regard, so her presence there as a housekeeper would have to be explained by Minnie's clever words, and she now lived in the Hall as the woman's own daughter . . . It could actually work, couldn't it? The servants had always liked her, the ones that had known her from being a child, so why would anyone deliberately reveal her? Besides there were so few left. Visitors might be a problem, but then Mrs. Hitchins was always invisible on such occasions, so why could she not be? It would only be for a few months and autumn and winter meant fewer visitors anyway. No, this could work very well. If not, then at worst she would be thrown out. Then she would travel to Bath earlier!

'Well, Mrs. Avery, you had better acquaint yourself with Mrs. Hitchins and she can show you the ropes.'

'Oh, it was I who trained, Mrs. Hitchins, sir,' Minnie said confidently. 'I'll make sure that the transition goes smoothly. And don't you worry, we'll be there when needed.' Minnie smiled but as Sir Christian spoke her smile faltered.

'Oh, Mrs. Avery will live within Kinsley Hall. A housekeeper needs to be in the house at all times. I will make sure that a room is made ready, and you will be comfortable. However, and I insist upon this, I cannot have my housekeeper running with muddy skirts back and fore from an estate cottage.'

Minnie's ruddy cheeks almost glowed. She had no argument to make against this because there was none to be had.

'Very well, sir,' Eleanor chipped in. 'I presume a room will be made available for Mrs. Jennings so on nights when the weather is foul, as you say, or you have guests and the eating is late, she will have a place to sleep near my own.'

It was Minnie's turn to look surprised.

'Of course, and that will not affect the entitlement to your delightful cottage, Mrs. Jennings,' he said politely as he replaced his hat.

Minnie nodded. 'Thank you,' she said, but before she stood up Eleanor had already opened the door to see him out.

He stepped over the threshold before glancing down into Eleanor's curious blue-green eyes.

'Have we met before, Mrs. Avery?' he said in a soft voice. Whatever thoughts had crossed his mind appeared to puzzle him. 'There is something familiar about you that I cannot quite place.'

'I do not think so, Sir Christian,' she answered honestly, for with his fine features, the strength of character that shone through those deep brown pools she would have remembered him well enough. Those striking eyes were now etched on her memory.

'Strange.' He shrugged, as if it had been a moment's fanciful notion. 'Very well, Mrs. Avery, come to the Hall tomorrow at noon and I will take you into Northallerton where you can be fitted for your uniform.'

'Yes, Sir Christian,' she said quietly as she watched him walk away. When she closed the door, she was greeted by Minnie's quizzical gaze.

Eleanor shrugged as if there was nothing to be done about it. Minnie shook her head. 'You should not be travelling alone with a single man who has no connection to you.'

'Perhaps not, but wouldn't Mrs. Avery be fine to travel alone with 'Sir' for the sake of a fitting for her new uniform, Minnie?'

The woman nodded back. 'I need my breakfast. And you, lass, need to take care. He's a handsome man, the right side of thirty I would guess, but he could also be trouble. We need to think and plan.'

8

Early the next morning Eleanor left her little, cosy bed. Soon she would be stepping back into her beautiful home.

Minnie met her in the kitchen.

'Remember, you are only helping out and do not let Sir Christian take advantage of you in any way. Just quietly go about the place as if you are familiar with it, but not like you own it. Ellie, are you listening to me?' Minnie asked as they walked briskly out of the door heading for the east gate of the walled garden.

'Yes, Mrs. Jennings, of course I am. As any housekeeper would her trusted cook.' Eleanor laughed at the cutting side-ways glance she received.

'This is not a joking matter, miss. We have no idea what the man is like, and you are going to have to live a shadow-life keeping your true identity a secret, until you have retrieved all you need, for we know not what he would do if the truth was known. He did not purchase you with the property or win ownership. He must never think that. You are in a very vulnerable situation, but if you can keep this position in safety for a few months, you may be free and safe.' She shrugged. 'Don't ask me where. You have time to think and access your stationery so you can write folks, and hopefully someone will come good for you. If not, there is always my cottage, but Sir Christian found me so quickly. The door will always be open, but like he pointed out, I am in no position to speak against him if you sought refuge there without his approval.' Minnie looked far from happy as if she was having second and third thoughts.

'Do not worry, Minnie — sorry, I should get used to calling you Mrs. Jennings again. We shall take each day on its own merit as the good Lord taught us and see how things unfold.' She smiled, feeling strangely relieved to be going home. Yet Minnie was quite correct, the man could be a positive ogre and then she would be trapped. She thought of his dark features and the glint that had sparked in his eyes when she had unwittingly asked him for his card, and her instinct told her he was not a man to fear. There again, Eleanor had never feared Jemima and perhaps she should have.

They arrived at the Hall early enough for them to have a fine breakfast using the kitchen's supplies whilst the remaining staff were otherwise occupied about their duties.

'Now, Ellie . . .' Minnie began, but Eleanor had been letting Minnie's chattering wash over her, lost to her own thoughts and plans. One point she had to discover was how to move her writing box and the trunk she had stored in the old nursery cupboard out of the Hall and into the cottage safely without being seen. He may be married! The thought snapped her back to reality. The prospect upset her more than it should do. They had not even asked if he lived alone. A woman would be curious and look in every room of her newly acquired home.

'That is the problem, Mrs. Jennings, I never have owned the Hall, or we would not be in the pickle we are in now. You had better get used to calling me Mrs. Avery in front of people and only use Ellie in the cottage. Or our little ruse will be shattered before it has begun. If 'Sir Christian' hears you calling me Miss Eleanor, he will become suspicious.'

'You make a fair point. Perhaps, Mrs. Avery,' Minnie chuckled, 'you could use some of that learning to help me make a full inventory of the kitchen's store-rooms. Looks like they've been kept organised, and a deal underused by Mrs. Hitchins and the maid, whilst Lady Jemima left with what she could carry. It could be she cleaned them out, but I doubt it. More like let them run down leaving Mrs. Hitchins with little variety to live off.'

Eleanor took the opportunity to leave on a task of her own and to begin going through the linen cupboard.

'Ah, Gertie! Glad to see you again, lass!' Minnie looked up and greeted Mrs.

Hitchins with a warm hug and smile; her enthusiasm was reciprocated. Obviously, the burden of being the only member of staff with any position of authority was too much for Mrs. Hitchins. Together they went through the much-depleted stores with almost military precision.

'Oh, Minerva, how much I have missed your lovely company. Sir Christian asked me to make a list of the staff and the supplies needed to get the Hall running properly again. I did try, but my heart breaks for the life we had before all of this nightmare unfolded. Can you look over this and let me know if I've missed anyone off?' The woman came in and sat down at the table where there was already tea placed ready for her. When Eleanor returned looking quite stern, Mrs. Hitchin's anxious head spun around, and she instantly stood up.

'Sit your body down, Gertie. She won't bite. Besides, we need your help also.' Minnie winked as the woman slunk down into the chair again.

'Mrs. Jennings?' she queried, her back

ramrod straight her expression showing her confusion.

'Please relax, Mrs. Hitchins, I am no longer here as a daughter of the Hall. My position did not protect me from being cast out like the staff.' Eleanor heard the bitterness creeping into her own voice and did not like it. She was not naturally a bitter person and had no wish to become one, so she smiled politely at the nervous face of Mrs. Hitchins, 'The linen cupboard has been somewhat depleted too.'

'Well, that is no surprise. Fortunately for you, lass, you were not cast far and now fate has brought you back here nice and safe.' Minnie looked at her with more than a little note of rebuke in her voice.

'I am more than grateful for your hospitality, Mrs. Jennings. I did not mean to sound as though I was not. Forgive me, please.' She saw a look of approval cross Mrs. Hitchins' face.

'Accepted! Here, set yourself on that stool and I'll fix your hair and let's get that ribbon straight on your lovely straw bonnet. Then you can travel into Northallerton looking respectable, like a lady should do. No one must suspect that you are any less than you were, if you catch my meaning.' Minnie winked at Mrs. Hitchins.

Eleanor took her seat as requested whilst Minnie filled Mrs. Hitchins in on the details regarding her new employment. With eyes wide and mouth munching a piece of parkin, Mrs. Hitchins listened intently as she savoured the warmth of the ginger spice within the cake's bake.

'So, you will keep house for him just until a proper housekeeper is found,' Mrs. Hitchins said.

'Yes, precisely that,' Eleanor said quickly, deciding that this was a far more plausible explanation than admitting she was planning to live there under subterfuge for the foreseeable future. If word got out, to anyone who cared to gossip, it could also be plausible as she was helping Sir Christian amicably, with her own future still in abeyance, with Mrs. Jennings as her chaperone like she had been for her mother. Their plan was gaining depth.

'And then he will find you a suitable position elsewhere? A governess or companion, yes — that would be good like our Minnie was to your own mother. That worked very well as she has her own cottage now big enough to house a small family.' Mrs. Hitchins nodded at Minnie as if it was the perfect solution.

'Yes, something like that would be most suitable, I am sure,' Eleanor said and looked at Minnie who raised one eyebrow, knowing Eleanor was making up a story that Mrs. Hitchins could happily accept.

'Well, that's for the future. For now, you must present yourself in the entrance hall and wait for Sir Christian to greet you. Eleanor, I am glad that you decided to wear your blue spencer. It is a beautiful shade and sets off your eyes well. You do not want 'Sir' to think you a simple country wench.' Minnie smiled.

'Goodness, how could he when she was born and bred a lady of this Hall. He is a brusque, ex-army man, but he does not strike me as vulgar just, well . . . opinionated and rather headstrong. Yet, that spencer is hardly the garb of a housekeeper, even a temporary one,' Mrs. Hitchins said.

'Precisely, Gertie! We want him to value Eleanor and the way she is going to help him out,' Minnie added quickly. 'Of course, she should dress appropriately. Like you said, he is a fine-looking, young man who has the responsibility of Kinsley Hall resting on his broad shoulders. He will need someone equal to the task of running his new home.'

Mrs. Hitchins and Minnie exchanged a knowing nod, which Eleanor did not quite understand, but felt there was a meaning behind their words.

'What do I tell him if he asks how even a temporary servant is wearing such a quality garment?' Eleanor glanced at Mrs. Hitchins' face as she was obviously trying hard to follow why he should not know the reason.

'Miss Eleanor,' Mrs. Hitchins said simply, 'you tell the man the truth of it and let his conscience be his guide. You should have been able to go to your Aunt Amelia in Northallerton and were callously turned away. He must have some endearing quality for has he not re-employed Mrs. Jennings and taken you under his wing?' She nodded to strengthen the truth of her words.

'Exactly, Gertie . . .'

'Minerva, please call me Gertrude; you know I hate the abridged version of my name.' She flinched as it upset her.

'Very well, Gertrude, as long as you call me 'Minnie' for I hate the proper one given me by my father who thought himself better than he was, because he had been blessed with the name Montgomery — and he a simple tanner!' She shook her head.

Eleanor smiled as 'Gertrude' turned her nose up at the thought of the odours relating to this very messy, yet important, profession.

'My father was a curate; he was to be a priest but, alas, died of consumption one horrid winter. I became a governess and then housekeeper,' Mrs. Hitchins admitted. Eleanor did not quite know how to respond.

'Go, Miss Eleanor, and attend Sir Christian, for you want to show that you are punctual, reliable and, importantly, polite.' Minnie walked with her to the end of the servants' corridor. 'Remember, though, try not to lie outright, but evade the truth for as long as possible. No use rubbing salt into an erstwhile healing wound; you are here temporarily for you cannot be here for the Christmas ball, if that tradition is to be upheld. Not as his housekeeper anyway, so you have a few months in hand to impress him and collect your things so that arrangements can be made for you to move safely on. If necessary, that is.'

'Of course, it will be necessary. How on earth can I stay?' Eleanor said.

'Well, trust in God, lass, for if there is a way, he'll set you on it.'

'Very well, Mrs. Jennings, I will do as you bid!' Eleanor hugged the woman to her, making Minnie chuckle at the gesture. 'Thank you for helping me,' she said and humbled by this moment of gratitude, left quickly entering the main entrance by the door that she had hardly ever ventured through before.

She made her way to the morning room, as she would normally do when she was kept waiting for Horace or Jemima to arrive, forgetting completely about waiting discreetly in the entrance as she had been instructed.

She stood looking out of the tall window, watching the sheep grazing in the fields that bordered the drive. Quietly overwhelmed by the beauty and simplicity of this familiar scene, she breathed in deeply and thanked God for this moment, which she thought had been stolen from her forever.

She did not have to wait for long.

'Ah, Mrs. Avery, there you are . . .' He walked in holding his tall hat and cane in one hand as he glanced up, his attention had been on straightening the collar of his riding coat as he entered. When he took in Eleanor's form he stopped in his tracks.

Eleanor faced him; her own gloved fingers were casually interlocked in front of her buttoned spencer. The high collar served to hide some of the colour that spread across her cheeks when she realised the effect her appearance was having on him. She was either in the wrong place, or he found her slender figure appealing. The latter thought pleased her for the feeling was unexpectedly mutual.

'Yes, Sir Christian,' she said in order to break the awkward silence that had formed between them. His eyes fixed on the brocade that surrounded the buttoned fastening of her coat below her neckline. The high waist helped to give her a long, leaner appearance. Whereas the spencer hugged her arms from above the elbow to her dainty wrists. It was her favourite, and she wore it well.

'I am glad you are punctual!' His words

were stark. Clearing his throat Christian turned away. 'Should we?' he asked and gestured she should walk out of the door and make for the coach.

'Yes, we should,' she said, nodding slightly as she confidently passed by him.

She descended the five entrance steps, breathing in the chill of the air, and waited as the driver of a fine coach unfolded the step so that she could climb into the carriage. He was a stocky man, of powerful build, his eyes seeming to take in everything about her without staring directly. Eleanor had not seen him before, which was a relief for he would not know who she was either.

'Bill, did you have any joy in Wetherby?' Christian asked as she made herself comfortable in the coach. Then she remembered that Mrs. Hitchins was not to travel with them. She could have been included as the current housekeeper, to act as a chaperone to Eleanor, couldn't she? But Eleanor was not there as a lady but as a servant. The thought excited her, but she must not be seen alone in a coach with this man by her aunt in Northallerton.

'Some, sir,' his manservant replied, addressing him as though he was still a senior officer, 'I shall take up where I left off whilst you and the young lady see to your business.' He smiled, which softened his war hardened face.

'Very good,' Christian replied.

Eleanor sat inside the coach, which with its gold velvet cushions was finer than Kinsley Hall's old leather covered ones. She looked back at the Hall anxiously as Christian placed his foot on the step of the coach ready to enter.

She leaned forward. 'Are we not waiting for Mrs. Hitchins to accompany me . . . us . . .' she asked. Eleanor should have heeded Minnie's warning.

'She does not need a new outfit, Mrs. Avery. She chose to leave her position if you recall.' He was poised with one foot on the step and one still on the ground.

'Yes, but . . . you and I are not acquainted and . . .' Panic began to rise.

'And it is a damned windy day, and

unlike my man Bill, I am not disposed to stand against the elements as I have no intention on riding atop my own damned coach!' He pushed his way in and dropped into the seat before shutting the door firmly and tapping the roof of the coach with his cane. The vehicle moved forward with a sudden lurch, although he had given her the courtesy of sitting forward facing. She stared out of the window.

'So, tell me how you know the Hall so well and how long you have lived there.' He placed his hat on the seat next to him and balanced his hands atop the cane as the coach bobbed and lurched along.

'I have lived here for quite a while, but . . .' Eleanor struggled for the right words to say. Minnie said stay near the truth when lying. 'I have lived in the area all my life . . .'

He laughed at her. She stopped watching the sheep in the field and stared directly at him.

'What do you find so amusing, Sir Christian?' she asked.

'You, 'Mrs. Avery', for I am delighted to learn that you are an atrocious liar!'

Eleanor regarded the smug expression on his face with a growing doubt in her mind — what was he thinking?

9

‘You insult me, Sir Christian!’ The carriage traversed a rut in the road, and she fell forward, which broke Eleanor’s moment of indignation as one hand flew to hold her hat, the other to steady herself by grabbing the door handle.

He sat as steady as a rock, balancing both hands atop the cane, his booted feet firmly planted on the coach floor at either side of it. The blackthorn cane had a striking silver wolf’s head engraved on its handle. Like its owner, it looked strong and determined.

‘No, Miss Eleanor, you insult my intellect. If your clothes were not too grand for you to have served in anyone else’s house, your manner and expectations certainly would be.’ He shook his head when she parted her lips to deny his accusation.

‘Very well, I shall not insult you further, as it was never my intention. It is true I have not always been in need of taking a position. In fact, this is the first one I will have entertained the thought of, but I am content to be your housekeeper and help you in the transition as owner of Kinsley.' She tried hard to remain calm and retain a voice of some authority.

He laughed. 'That is exceptionally good of you. I feel so honoured,' hardly able to contain the sarcasm that filled his every word.

It was so tempting to reply that he should be. Instead, she pursed her lips together and composed herself. Eleanor really did not want to lose the chance to live for at least a while longer in her own home. Please, Eleanor thought, do not let me end up thrown back onto my aunt's merciless scorn. She could hardly stay on this man's estate, even in Minnie's cottage, if she openly challenged him.

'Is there anything else you would like to tell me now, 'Miss Eleanor', before you leave this coach as Mrs. Avery, embracing a new beginning and challenge for such a fine young lady as yourself? I wonder how easy you will humble yourself into the position.' He continued to stare at her. 'Will I find myself living with a harridan keeping a strict house and making demands upon how I run my own household?'

Eleanor fought to control her posture: proud and strong; her manner: genteel, not submissive, and her words: polite but undeterred. 'You flatter my ability and desire to control you, anything, or anyone for that matter. Do you not understand the position I have found myself in? As many other young ladies of good family, I am in reduced circumstances, not of my own making. I have no wish to become a harridan, nor see the need for it. I can, however, run a smooth and efficient household for you.' Having stated her opinion, she looked outside at the beauty of the wild moors as the horses pulled the carriage up the steep bank. She could hear the driver shouting encouragement at the animals to push them onward. Soon they would be on what was thought to be a road-built centuries earlier by Roman soldiers. The majesty of the moors was never lost on her as, even in a coach as fine as this one, she felt so small and vulnerable by comparison to the wilderness outside.

'How did you come to find yourself in such a position?' he asked. 'Help me to understand, as you appear to think that it is beyond me.'

Eleanor did not look back at him until he tapped her knee gently with his cane. Instantly her head shot round.

'Thank you. It is not polite to address the side of someone's head, or so I was taught by one of my governesses, if I remember my lessons well.' He waited for her reply.

'I was admiring beauty, sir,' Eleanor explained, whilst trying to empty her mind of how she came to find herself confined with such a handsome stranger. Her head wanted to hate him, but her heart seemed to be having a different reaction.

'So was I but having now studied your elegant profile I would like to hear your honeyed words explain how you came to be in this situation.'

Eleanor was taken aback by his statement — honeyed indeed! She was not so easily taken in by a few flattering words. 'I became a burden to my widowed sister-in-law and well . . . it was apparently inconvenient for my aunt to house me, so I really was left little option.' Happy that she had not lied, or even embellished the truth, Eleanor sat back as the carriage levelled at the top of the bank.

He nodded and paused as if contemplating his next words.

'That is true. I give you full credit, Miss Eleanor, for having a stronger character and a clearer head than that sad excuse of a brother of yours.' His face was set, words direct and body still.

Silence grew between them.

'You speak ill of the dead, so easily.' Eleanor did not deny his assumption. He clearly knew who she was.

'Yes, because I speak the truth and you did not deny it either.'

Eleanor was shocked; he knew all! 'If you were aware that my brother was Horace . . . , why did you not say straight away? How did you know?' Eleanor stared, disbelief and fear undermining the façade she had built for their charade they had only just begun, and it had seemed to be going so well!

'You bear a striking family resemblance to Horace; the colour of your hair, the light green blue of your eyes and the undeniable fact that you stepped into Kinsley Hall as if it was your own. Did you really think that for a second I would not suspect you were an imposter to the rank?'

She swallowed and tried to control the moisture that threatened to spill from her beautiful eyes and roll down her cheeks.

'Will you still accept my offer to be your housekeeper?' She clasped both hands together and rested them on her lap to steady her trembling feelings.

There was no shame, Eleanor told herself. At least she would be in her own home.

'No,' he said simply.

Her hand shot to her mouth. Was she destined to live her days cossetted away with Minnie? 'But why? I know the place better than anyone and instructed Mrs. Hitchins,' she said. 'You could do a lot worse, and I promise not to forget my new place.' Humble, she must stay humble, she tried.

'Because, Miss Eleanor, I made a promise to your brother when I visited him in his Paris garret before he parted this world. It is one that I wondered how I was to honour when I had heard the family had already left for the county of Kent. I had not realised you had been cast off rather than swept away with the family carriage. Perhaps Horace knew his wife better than you may have realised.' He shrugged and shook his head. 'How lovely his 'lady' wife must be. Then you opened the door of Briar cottage to me, a rare English rose indeed and, the very one I was about to trace. How strange fate is.'

'What promise was that?' she asked, her words little more than a whisper. She did not dare voice her thoughts on Jemima lest he think she did not deserve the description of 'a lady' either.

'To find you a suitable husband.' He stared at her as his words sank in.

'Well, you can be relieved of that burden for I am certain I will find one myself.' She replied hastily, she had no idea how unless she met a farmhand. 'I do not need a total stranger to burden himself so, not on my behalf!' She felt panic rise within, her hands shook, hopefully not obviously, as her grip tightened.

'By being my housekeeper, wearing a dour dress and living in the shadows, being called Mrs. Avery?' He chuckled. 'You have as much chance of finding a suitable husband like that as Napoleon did of defeating the British.'

She breathed deeply, cheeks burning as the first houses of Northallerton came into view. She must stay calm.

'Love finds a way . . . You should have more faith, Sir Christian. Horace was obviously delirious because you did not even know me, and he would not leave my future to a stranger's whim!'

'Love! You think love enters into this equation at all?' He shook his head. 'You need to be looked after, provided for and I intend to make sure that this happens. Has it occurred to you that on his dying bed Horace thought so highly of me that he would entrust me to perform this task? To be the honourable and trustworthy man that he could never be?'

'You have no authority over me, my life!' she said as confidently as she could.

'That is where you are wrong, Miss Eleanor, for I have absolute authority over you. Horace made me your guardian. You are but twenty years and I am about to take you to my legal advisors where papers confirming my ownership of Kinsley Hall and my agreement regarding your guardianship will be confirmed. You will be advised as to your options, but then you must for your own safety see sense and stay where I place you.'

'But . . . but . . . I . . .'

'You will temporarily run my household, whilst we are without a housekeeper, but you will continue to dress as one befitting your rank. I cannot abide a dour figure stalking the Hall like a ghost. You can help me re-engage the staff needed. You will be able to live in your own rooms, see your loyal servant Mrs. Jennings by overseeing the menus for the week ahead, and be hostess at any social gathering that is held. However, you will not make arrangements to leave the Hall without my permission, you will not invite guests to it without my approval, you will have a limit on the amount paid for your wardrobe, but there will be one — an allowance that is — and you shall be made aware of when I am at the Hall and when I shall be away and when I require your company to attend functions elsewhere.'

Eleanor gathered her wits as she

absorbed this new situation. 'Did you encourage Horace to gamble away the Hall? She asked as her mind tried to absorb this new turn of events.

'I won it fairly — your brother gambled all and lost.'

Eleanor gaped at him open mouthed for a moment, he made it seem so unfeeling. How could Horace have been so irresponsible? To leave them all without a home, except of course he had made some arrangements for her with this man . . .

'You are quite mistaken, Sir Christian.' Eleanor thought the man's success at the gaming table, taking the estate from an ailing man, had gone to his head. 'If Horace had left any legal arrangements, then I should have been told of them by now. Jemima was brought the sad news by Horace's legal representative, and he did not even speak to me. Therefore, I have every right to make up my own mind what happens next!'

Christian placed the cane along the floor of the carriage and folded his arms across his chest stretching the sleeves of his jacket over muscular arms. 'Lady Jemima has much to answer for I'm afraid and, believe me, she will. Not only has she stolen a carriage that did not belong to her, but she has denied you the chance to understand your situation. In short, you could have been ruined. Your aunt, should she have offered, could have taken on your guardianship for an allowance. However, I gather you were turned away, so she was unaware of this also. In the absence of her goodwill the task has fallen to me. I do not intend to relinquish it.'

'But why? What do you gain by keeping me at the Hall?' Eleanor asked.

'Gain? You really have no idea of honour, do you?' He shook his head. 'Haven't I just explained to you that I gave my word to a dying man?' he asked.

'One that you stole away an inheritance from!' Her hands balled into fists as she leaned forward pushing them down into the cushions.

'Silence!' the word was snapped out

causing Eleanor to instantly regret her foolish outburst, she recoiled 'I . . .'

'You will never accuse me of that again. A fool challenged me, and I beat him fairly with witnesses present. Nothing was done to steal or cheat the man. In fact, I tried to stop him, but he was so adamant that his fortunes were about to change. So do not deride me ever again.' His tone and face were stern. A man used to being obeyed.

Eleanor sat calmly, knowing she had spoken out of anger and had no call to accuse Sir Christian of being a cheat, yet he was a stranger who wielded such power over her future.

'I am telling you what will happen. Do not besmirch my good character.' His voice was now quite mellow, not angry.

'I was too harsh, I admit that, but you must see that the consequences of that gamble changed the course of my life irrevocably?' She replaced her hands on her lap. A tremble began again, but she could not blubber like a child. What had been done, had been done.

‘Yes, I see that, as it has mine. Yours was already heading in a very downward direction, though. Now I can open new and more attractive options for you. We shall arrive shortly. So please listen for I will only have this discussion once. I won your home fair and square. If your mutton-headed brother had not been so reckless I would have let the game pass me by, but there were dishonourable men present who would have taken his Hall and you, keenly.’

‘You are telling me you did it as a gesture of goodwill. Pray, if you are so saintly in your actions then why did you not hand it back to him the next day?’ Eleanor was angry and knew she sounded bitter again.

‘I claimed my prize. It fitted, my regiment was disbanding, I wanted a new challenge. Besides, the only other possession he could offer up — he did so willingly enough.’

‘That being?’ she asked.

‘You, Miss Eleanor! Your care, your guardianship. He showed those present your miniature portrait which I glimpsed. I took his challenge and won the prize.' He watched her shock penetrate but sat still.

His words slowly seeped into her unwilling thoughts. She had been as good as auctioned, but Horace had not gained anything from the deal. He had literally thrown his inheritance and his sister away. Jemima and Quentin had escaped to Kent. But she was trapped in the Hall with a strange man who thought he had a legal claim upon her. How impossible a situation! How was she to break free now?

'How did he die?' she asked focussing on her lap, trying to change the conversation, whilst she pondered what had happened. How much her life had changed.

'He drank himself into a stupor, contracted pneumonia. He pleaded with me on his death bed to find you a suitable match.' He shrugged. 'I thought your character must be plain, dull or mischievous for your relative not to want you. However, I see that you are quite becoming in looks, you seem to have an interesting, reasonably honest character, so I shall happily honour his request and see you wed.'

'I have said that is not necessary.' Eleanor was adamant.

'And I gave my word and that I will not break. This conversation has ended.'

'Oh, has it?' Petulance was not becoming and yet she found his manner triggered an equally strong reaction. How was she to simply accept his influence on her life?

By this time, the coach had drawn to a halt. The two stared at each other defiantly, neither wanting to break the deadlock.

Bill opened the carriage door and cleared his throat audibly. 'Sir, Mrs. Avery.' He lowered the step and stood back. Christian collected his hat and placed it upon his raven hair as he alighted and picked up his cane. His hand was proffered for Eleanor to take. She did not want to. She wanted to open the other door and run off into the narrow alleyways to lose herself and find solitude somewhere, perhaps All Saint's, where she could pray for help — guidance as to what to do — but she dared not. Reluctantly she held his hand just long enough to alight from the carriage without losing her balance. The man, Bill, was looking from one to the other. Whoever he was, it seemed he weighed her up and yet still surveyed the people passing by. To her amazement he winked at her when Sir Christian was not aware.

Eleanor straightened her back and relaxed her shoulders before taking her first step into a very different future.

10

They entered through the old door passing black timbers that looked stark against the whitewashed walls.

Inside, the smell of lamps and candles mingled with that of old papers, ink, leather, and velum. With the heavy scent of the musk that filled the air from the male clerks that worked at high desks in a room to her left, the place was somewhat airless.

They were escorted into a small office by a clerk. Unable to turn away and walk out, she dutifully followed Christian's lead. A man in a powdered wig, a serious expression and a precariously balanced monocle stood as they entered. Christian was careful to allow her to walk in front of him and into the room where she took a seat.

'Please be seated, Sir Christian,' the man said. Christian assumed his seat facing the gentleman, as did she, in front of his paper covered desk. It seemed busy, rather than disorderly.

'Now, Sir Christian, I am glad to learn that you have actually located Miss Eleanor.' The man favoured her with a stern and disapproving look.

'I did not have to search far, Mr Copeland, she was in the care of her mother's faithful companion being looked after on the estate. I am amazed that your man did not manage to seek her out and inform her of the arrangements that have been made. He seems to have only dealt with the lady of the Hall, ignoring Miss Eleanor's concern and interest in the situation. Indeed, Miss Eleanor even held a conversation with your representative. He knew she was there!'

'Master Horace's good lady gave her word that she would break the sad news to her sister-in-law in a gentle way. We had no reason to doubt her word,' Mr Copeland replied firmly.

'This lady was believed, rather than the man stay and do his legal duty. Lady

Jemima then left with my carriage and four fine horses,' Christian added to stress his point.

'Well, when we were advised that Miss Eleanor had left the Hall via a note from Lady Jemima, and we enquired with her aunt who had no knowledge of her whereabouts, it was then that both she, and ourselves, became most concerned for her.'

'Was that when you told her aunt that a provision for her care had been offered in exchange for the inconvenience?' Sarcasm dripped from Christian's tongue, but the man shuffled papers and then stared defiantly back at him. He was not used to having his professionalism challenged, that was clear even to Eleanor.

Mr Copeland coloured deeply, but his gaze did not flicker.

'I will not live with my aunt,' Eleanor said, breaking her silence.

Mr Copeland glared at her. 'My dear, think of what you are saying. You have left yourself in a precarious position.

If you have been seen alighting from that coach with Sir Christian, a virtual stranger to you, your reputation has already been damaged, even if we can find a plausible explanation for where you have been whilst coming to terms with your grief. Do you mean to willingly allow this man as your guardian to find you a husband? Your aunt's guardianship is the only alternative.'

His words were stark, showing more a desire to go against Sir Christian's wishes than be genuinely concerned for Eleanor. Her aunt also used this legal practice; she knew that from when her uncle, her lovely fun-loving uncle, had died a year since.

'I am stating that I shall not live with my aunt. She turned me away when I visited her; she denied this as she denied me too.' Eleanor swallowed.

'I presume you are speaking from an emotional state and not with a logical mind. Women are fickle creatures.' His attention refocussed solely on Christian, dismissing Eleanor with his comment.

'Very well, Sir Christian, you are prepared to find a suitable match for this young woman. Her reputation may already be slightly besmirched, besides which she does not have a dowry of note and has been cast off by her family.'

Eleanor shook her head. Offended, with no point in trying to argue her case, she was going to stand and walk out. Life with Minnie would be preferable to this.

Christian placed his hand on her arm and stopped her. Was he able to read her mind, she wondered?

'Yes, I already have someone of note in mind,' Christian said.

Eleanor stiffened.

'Very well, here are the papers, you can sign here, and the account will be settled.'

'Can I read the papers?' Eleanor asked.

'No, that would be most irregular . . . your signature is not required.' Mr Copeland protested.

'Let her, then there can be no doubt in Miss Eleanor's mind that all is as we have said.'

Eleanor read the document, not understanding some of the legal terms, but loath to ask the men for further clarification. Yet those that she did understand made it clear that Kinsley Hall was now the estate of Sir Leigh-Bolton in its entirety. Revoking all other claims to the properties upon it, she pointed to this clause, and asked, 'Briar Cottage?'

Mr Copeland jumped in. 'That is a bequest which will be honoured but other tenant agreements can be revised. They should be updated or withdrawn. No family member can make claim as the estate was . . .'

'Won fair and square . . .' Christian chipped in.

'Legally claimed by Sir Christian with your brother's agreement,' Mr Copeland finished.

'Enough!' Christian took hold of the pen and signed the forms. 'Let it be known that I am now Miss Eleanor's legal guardian and that should squash all gossip when we are seen together about town. Come, Eleanor, we shall see your outfitter and then take lunch.' Christian stood up and walked out.

Eleanor did likewise, her legs struggling to move for a moment as the enormity of what had just happened hit her hard. Mr Copeland stood once more and gave a small bow in Eleanor's direction. 'You best do his bidding, Miss Eleanor, you just gave him absolute power over you instead of returning humbly to your poor, confused aunt.' He shook his head dismissively.

Eleanor dug deep to find her strength. Straightening her shoulders and with her head high she walked out to find the carriage gone and Sir Christian waiting for her. It was hard to judge his expression, but it seemed to be one that was pleased with the day's events.

Who had he in mind as a suitor for her? Had he really just won her along with the estate?

11

Eleanor walked alongside him in silence. Sir Christian led her to a dressmaker's shop. A bell rang as they entered which snapped Eleanor out of her daze. A lady in a marine blue dress approached, the fine quality white lace that edged her dress was a stark contrast but immaculately made and starched.

'Can I be of assistance?' she asked, eyeing Sir Christian appreciatively, Eleanor thought.

'Yes, my ward needs three new outfits: a fine gown for dinner parties, a warmer walking dress and pelisse, hats and boots and a complete set of riding attire.'

Eleanor stood there watching the shopkeeper's eyes widen. She hoped her own expression was more controlled.

'If you fulfil this order to my satisfaction then we shall open an account.'

The woman preened. 'Of course, our work is second to none. Leave your ward with us and we shall take all the required measurements. I have a book of fabrics that are available at the drapers from which choices can be made.' She looked at Eleanor. 'If you would come through, miss, we shall begin.'

'Good,' Sir Christian said. 'You may add on any bits and pieces as needed but not to excess, Miss Eleanor. I shall return in an hour.'

'Thank you,' she muttered and walked through to the back of the shop hearing the bell announce his departure. This was not her usual outfitter as it was considered too fancy for Eleanor by her brother and Jemima, although she suspected that her sister-in-law had frequented it often.

After an extremely busy but enjoyable hour Christian returned to her. She had been given sweet delicacies and the finest tea whilst choosing fabrics and accessories, this service where everything could be ordered from one place was a new experience for Eleanor. The money being spent on her could be part of her family's estate so why should she not make the most of the opportunity.

They left the shop, and he cupped her elbow. Her pulse quickened and a flush of warmth rushed to her cheeks at the very familiar gesture.

They stopped outside one of the many coaching inns, now boasting its services as a fine hotel with new extensions to the rear. Here travellers could stop and take refreshments between coach rides if travelling on to a further destination or stay and enjoy the area, its markets, fine racing track and amenities. The only thing it lacked unlike nearby Harrogate, was a natural spa.

Eleanor waited with her guardian to be seated in the dining room. She was in a place where she was known by some of Horace's society friends, with her escort, who, she presumed, was as unknown to them as he was to her. Eleanor glanced around at the surprisingly light dining room, which had been attractively decorated with pale cream plaster between the heavier, darkened wood beams.

She fought to keep a calm composure. His confident fashionable appearance pleased her greatly. If he were some years older perhaps, he could have been taken as a distant uncle figure. But he was unmistakably, splendidly handsome and in his prime.

Eleanor recognised a few faces from her brother's social set. Sir Thomas Ellerby was one such; she nodded politely across the room. He was seated with his wife but the astonishment on the man's face was clear. Their eyes were taking in every detail of Christian's fine bearing and apparel. Whispers were exchanged, their presence had been noted. This was a fashionable place to eat. Heads turned as they were escorted to a table, but Eleanor smiled confidently back as Christian chose a table in the centre of the dining room.

Once Christian was seated opposite, he ordered food for them both. His attention then returned to Eleanor who, confidence waning, was admiring the fine stitching on the napkin, wondering where to look next and trying hard not to colour and show how ill at ease she now felt.

'Eleanor,' he said in a voice that would not carry. 'This is a fine place to eat. I hope you enjoy the experience as my man informs me that only the best of people dine here.' He smiled, obviously finding humour in some private joke he had with Bill. For a master and servant, they were uncommonly close, Eleanor realised.

'Are you making a point, sir, or simply trying to embarrass me?' She sat upright, a strange feeling of daring and rebellion giving her false confidence. Eleanor just hoped it would hold. She had no wish to end up running out of a place like this in public shame.

'Which do you think?' he asked. He gestured for the waiter to come and serve them their wine.

'It is as if you are staking your claim in some way . . . You are announcing your arrival to the local society and that I am a part of the estate you have inheri . . . won,' she said, as the waiter returned with Christian's choice of wine. Christian took the bottle and carefully poured the wine into her crystal glass; sipping it rapidly she was surprised at its fine taste.

'Excellent, thank you,' Christian declared, and the waiter took his leave. He savoured and approved of the vintage before drinking a hearty mouthful. With a nod of the head, he acknowledged an acquaintance across the dining room. Perhaps he was not as unknown as she had thought!

'I am the lawful, rightful owner of Kinsley Hall and you are not to view yourself as part of my 'winnings', Miss Eleanor. You are from this day forth, and by your own agreement to it, my ward and rest therefore under my protection. We have nothing to hide from these people by being openly public about this. It is the swiftest way I could think of to spread our good fortune throughout the region, so let the gossips do their worst if they see fit to. We shall remain above it and shall enjoy our liberty.'

He was smiling with such ease that Eleanor realised he meant every word. This was not a charade to him. Concluding the meeting in the legal offices had taken a weight off his shoulders, he looked far less troubled and a few years younger as a result.

'You said that you had someone in mind for me, sir, a suitor, but you must accept that I do not wish . . .'

'Eleanor, that is for the future. Just enjoy the present. I want to know all about Kinsley, so do tell. You are a wealth of information on the subject because you were part of its past and shall now help to forge its future. Tell me who is the . . . ?'

'You have the gall to dine in here amongst civilised folks!' Sir Thomas Ellerby had stormed over to their table.

Eleanor replaced her wine glass lest her hand tremble and spill it, glancing at the surprised faces now staring at them absorbing the unfolding scene.

'Ellerby, won't you and your good lady

wife join us for dinner? Perhaps we could talk in a more commodious manner if you were seated at my table,' Christian offered.

'You bloody opportunist! You stole away a man's home, his legacy and his life!' His face filled with fury. 'And now you shame his sister with your presence!'

'Come now, Sir Thomas. Curb your language, please, there are ladies present. I think you are the one being shamed by your own ill-advised tongue.' Christian's voice was quiet and calm as he dismissed Ellerby's words with a wave of his hand. Fully aware that the man was on the verge of calling him out.

Eleanor swallowed. She did not want to look down in shame as she had done nothing wrong, neither did she want to stare across at the challenging faces delighting in the scene, or at Sir Thomas Ellerby, a man she had dined with in her home at many of Horace and Jemima's dinners. So, instead, she fixed her gaze upon Christian who seemed calm beyond measure. Could they leave now without looking cowed or disgraced, she wondered? Would he? Eleanor thought Christian's judgement of what actions of theirs were prudent to have fallen short on this occasion.

'I will not sit at a table with a thief!' Sir Thomas blustered, and a wave of gasps escaped from the diners immediately around them.

Christian stood up and looked down at the man, for he was a head and shoulder above him. 'You are misinformed, for your gambling friend, Sir Horace, was drinking himself into an early grave and betting recklessly. I saved Kinsley Hall from a far worse fate and have secured its future and this young lady's, who I am now honoured to act as guardian for. You, Ellerby, accuse me falsely! Now please either return to your table and your wife or join us but do sit down.' His words were loud enough to carry.

'Innocent, in whose eyes?' Sir Thomas demanded, both fists clenched by his side. His face looked fit to burst with indignation and yet Christian was not ruffled at all. His even composure helped Eleanor to keep her own.

'In the eyes of the law, sir, as it happens,' Christian said and raised a challenging eye. 'Would you see fit to challenge me in the courts if your feelings run so high on the matter? If so, I can give you the details of my solicitor now!'

Eleanor saw Sir Thomas' knuckles whiten and she honestly believed that he was going to call Christian out, but one man was used to a life of leisure and sport at the tracks and gaming tables, whilst the other was recently returned from commanding men at war. There would be no even challenge for him to face.

'You, sir . . .' Sir Thomas spluttered.

'Are hungry and here is our pheasant, so please, join us or leave. You are embarrassing your good lady wife,' Christian said, and sat back down, his attention returning to their food that had been placed by an anxious waiter on the centre of the table.

Sir Thomas stormed back to his table

and threw some money down upon it before ordering his wife to leave with him. Eleanor felt sorry for her, the lady did not know where to look, her face cast down as she scurried to the door following her husband, leaving a dinner half eaten. Sir Thomas passed by their table and meant to topple the wine bottle with his cane so it would spill on Christian's lap, but Christian's reflexes were too quick for him; he caught it before it had hardly moved. The infuriated man blustered out.

Christian smoothly refilled Eleanor's glass before the waiter began serving food onto her plate. Eleanor looked closely at Christian in amazement at how composed he had been throughout the whole embarrassing scene. The people around them soon lost interest and began chatting to each other again, seemingly not about them. The moment had passed. Christian started eating. Eleanor had not realised she had frozen in time like a statue.

'Ellie!' the quiet tone of Christian's

voice brought her attention back to him. 'Pick up your knife and fork and start eating, please.'

'Sorry,' she said and did as he asked, and as the motions prompted feelings of hunger and thirst, she realised that time began to move at its normal pace again. People finished their meals and left, some cast cool glances their way, others were ones of admiration. Christian smiled amicably back or gave a polite nod of acknowledgement as he sipped his wine. If he cared at all for the derisive looks or the odd caustic comment, he did not show it.

They finished their meal uninterrupted and in relative silence. The food had been like the wine — exquisite. The company had definitely been most entertaining. She had never cared for Sir Thomas Ellerby, finding him loud and coarse, always used to having his own way. His poor wife must have a life of hell, she thought.

* * *

'Well, Ellie, are you going to admonish me too?' he asked once they were seated in the carriage again.

'No, I will not. For the law is on your side, even if it appears word has spread that you are no more than an opportunistic rake!' She had not meant to add on the last comment, but he was handsome, he knew it, and some of the looks he attracted from the ladies present in the dining room were subtly flirtatious. One had even dropped her card casually into his lap as she left.

'A rake! Lady, your mouth has done you a disservice. Did I drink to excess? Have I been coarse? Do you know me to be a womaniser who has evil desires upon your virtue?' Christian goaded her, but she felt as if he were being as an annoying sibling, teasing her.

Eleanor shrank back a little into the soft cushions when he laughed at her.

'What to do with you?' he shook his head.

'Are you any of those things? Were you ever?' she asked.

‘No, I am not, and yes, some I have been, but I am no destroyer of innocence. You are safe to sleep in your bed at night without fear of me.’ He looked out of the window. ‘I will find peace here and I will not court the favour of those who hypocritically aim to condemn me, for they may well have had their share of good fortune from your brother’s poor skills at the gaming tables whilst buoying him up to carry on. I saw him and can assure you that Sir Thomas Ellerby is more than guilty of being a party to Horace’s downfall, but his ultimate fall was by his own hand, and we all have to be man enough to own our mistakes.’

‘So, when will you tell me who you have in mind for me as a suitor, sir, because I will not be forced to marry against my will?’ Eleanor declared and saw his brow crease.

‘I had to say something, and I actually do have a notion, but for now, please just let me re-establish Kinsley Hall as a manor house and a profitable working farm and help me to know the people on the estate. You shall not be forced into any match against your will, on that you have my word. But I have told you what I expect of you: you will keep house, you will be a hostess as I am single now, and you will ask me before venturing out. I am happy for you to carry on your life as you would normally, but you will not do anything outside the estate without my permission for your own safety; on this there is no exception.'

Eleanor nodded yet made no promises. 'I have not given you permission to call me Ellie.'

'No, do I need it when we are out of anyone else's earshot?'

'I suppose not,' she said without looking at him. It had a warm sound to it, or perhaps it was the effect his words were having upon her.

'Do you have a fiancée?' she asked.

'Heavens no!' he said. She had caught him off guard. He had not expected such a bold question. 'Why do you ask?' That humoured glint returned to his eyes.

'You mentioned 'as you were single'

. . . now. I presumed you intended to marry.'

'Oh, dear Ellie, never presume,' he winked at her then changed the subject again, 'Very well, Ellie, when we return home, please tell your accomplices that the truth is known about who you really are, and I will not tolerate any further subterfuge. However, I forgive all involved this time as their defence of you is quite touching and shows loyalty, a trait I value highly.'

'They only wanted to protect me . . .' Eleanor began to defend her friends, but he held up his hand to stop her, he had told her he understood so she kept her silence. So strange to realise she had thought of them as friends and not as servants.

'From what — the opportunist and rake that I am?' he asked opening his eyes wide, professing his innocence.

'From myself, Sir Christian, as I had to leave. I found that my aunt was not prepared to give me houseroom. Why? I have never wronged her. I have always been happy to see her, sing to or play pianoforte for her. Uncle and I were always so fond of each other. He was full of life and laughter. I miss him greatly.' She stopped talking for emotions began to bubble within for a family that had died out and beloved relatives that had left her — even her hapless brother.

'Perhaps that is it! You have youth, beauty, and talent. You represent things she can never possess again, and you also had captured her husband's heart. These things weigh heavily on a bitter widow's mind.' He shrugged, satisfied with his summation of the problem.

Eleanor did not speak. It seemed strange to her that the woman could have held such thoughts within and still smiled and greeted Eleanor when their family visited. How sad she must have been, living a constant lie.

12

Once out of the carriage Eleanor went straight to the walled garden. When she heard Christian take himself off on horseback with Bill, she ventured down to Briar Cottage where she found Minnie who had finished for the day as dinner was not required at the Hall.

Minnie stood as soon as she saw Eleanor. 'Well, tell me all . . . Gertrude said she would be over shortly, Eleanor.'

'As a plan it seems it fell short of being convincing,' Eleanor said slightly indignantly as she sat back down in the chair. She wondered where to begin.

'So, what happened? Did you break down and confess all to him in the coach as soon as those becoming eyes stared longingly into your own? Did he make you tell all, like some cad in a gothic novel?' Minnie asked, her face filled with curiosity mingled with disappointment, or possibly concern that her own situation could be impacted by her part in their naïve plan.

'No! Nothing like that. He knew who I was already. He realised as soon as I opened the door, for Horace and I had features in common. We never thought of that — our eyes. I am not so weak in character, Minnie, that I betray my friends easily. Besides, Horace did think of me in his final days and suggested that Sir Christian act as my legal guardian. Horace wished it so and he agreed, so that is that.' Eleanor swallowed but Minnie's eyes shone brighter than the stars.

'Goodness, lass! You will be the envy of every young maid in the county for he is such a fine-looking catch. Surely, he should know some equally handsome bucks to find you a decent suitor, in time, of course,' Minnie said and laughed. 'Eee, lass, you have landed on your feet!' She clasped her hands together in joy.

Eleanor did not quite share her enthusiasm. 'Perhaps, Minnie, we shall have to see. I will bide my time before deciding. For I have no wish to have a stranger find me any match at all.'

'Why ever not? You may well be surprised.' The annoying finger wagged at Eleanor, and she did not like it.

'He took over my home, Minnie, and so I will take what is mine from it as I planned to and leave as soon as I am able to have word sent to my good friends in Bath.' Eleanor felt reassured by having a plan, even if it was a very sketchy and unlikely one. It made her feel as though she still had some control over her own destiny.

'Lass, stop and think upon it. This is no simpleton with a title and a fat belly who has arrived at your door, but a fine-looking gentleman with contacts. This is an ex-army man who is in his prime. Do you not think he would hunt you down if you ran away? You go against him after he has secured the legal rights to care for you and you might find you have set yourself in conflict with an enemy who, when treated with some respect could have been your best friend. Go careful, dear Ellie. Whatever fond memories you have of the younger Master Horace, cast them aside for he grew into a man who was not noble and who left you extremely vulnerable. My advice to you is simple: give Sir Christian a chance to prove himself worthy of the estate and you.' Minnie waved an index finger at Eleanor, which was a gesture she was coming to strongly dislike.

'Hmm, I will collect my possessions and store them in my room, in readiness should I choose to leave,' Eleanor said defiantly.

Minnie stood up, hands on her hips. 'Have I ever told you about looking at a gift horse in the mouth?' Minnie asked.

'No, I don't remember you mentioning it,' Eleanor said and smiled.

'Then try!' Minnie snapped her words out as the door opened and a flustered Mrs. Hitchins burst in.

'What news, Miss Eleanor,' she asked.

Minnie shook her head at the flustered state of the woman. 'You best sit in me chair. I'll fetch you a tot of something calming. Ellie, explain the situation now, and don't go running on about the future. That is yet to come!'

13

The next few days were strangely exciting. Her new-found freedom to make decisions and plan to develop the gardens, hall and estate as she would have had it gave Eleanor such a sense of joy and contentment that she felt ashamed that she had ever proclaimed that she would make the new owner dread the day that he ever set foot inside Kinsley Hall.

Happily reunited with her personal belongings which Christian never questioned she felt more at peace and at home there than she ever had in her life.

She watched Christian returning along the drive and a smile crossed her face. He cut such a fine figure.

The image of an ogre she had painted of him in her mind's eye had been proven so untrue, even unjust.

Christian, with Bill, had visited each tenant farm in turn, listened to their grievances, and stated his expectations of them, agreeing to some overdue repairs.

He had written to Jemima and even bequeathed the coach to her for the good of Horace's son. The boy would have no claim on his father's lost inheritance, but Christian told Eleanor a sum had been settled in a trust to be used for the boy's education.

It was not guilt that had driven his decision, but a sense of fair play for it was hardly the child's fault that his father was so lacking in sense. As for Eleanor the more she enjoyed the life she had always craved at Kinsley the more her pity for Jemima's true loss had grown. The woman had not seen how to make this marvellous estate a home filled with love. Eleanor had no wish to invite her sister-in-law back and see her 'eat humble pie at their table'. Justice had already been done.

Eleanor's heart filled with the growing affection she could no longer deny as Christian entered the room. How could she ever give this up and settle for a man of his choosing as her husband?

It was true that she knew Christian would choose wisely, but not now — not ever for who could better the man who stood before her?

'Are you spying on me, Ellie?' he said as he picked up a delicacy from her plate by the window seat and savoured the sweetness of its pastry. 'Hmm, Cook puts our produce to excellent use.' He winked.

'I would make a very bad one if I stood in plain sight. No, I merely admired the horse's even gait.' She turned away as he laughed.

'Tomorrow, ride with me?' he was watching her closely.

'That would be excellent as I want to talk to you about the old weir. I think we could have it dredged and re-establish the water course at the bottom of the orchard. It would be made use of again and enhance the estate.'

He folded his arms across his chest and nodded.

'Very well we shall ride and talk about old rusty weirs and enjoy the fine weather. Have Cook prepare a small picnic and Bill can fetch it to us by the meadows to eat once we are done — talking.' He shook his head.

'That would also be . . .'

'Convenient?' he raised a brow.

'Quite lovely,' she admitted, fingering the ruby necklace she was now openly enjoying wearing.

'Good, you must learn to stop talking about horses, husbandry and engineering projects long enough to enjoy some life here, Eleanor,' he said.

'But I do . . . I enjoy it all,' she smiled. 'For as long as I am here, I will . . .' she let her words hang in the air, but he turned away glancing out of the window as Bill was also returning.

'Good,' he began to walk away. 'Then continue to do so.'

Eleanor did and two months flew by before she realised until the seasons began to turn once more, and the air cooled around her as her heart warmed to life in the only home she had ever known — the one where she belonged.

14

September 8th, 1816, Kinsley Hall

Eleanor had been allowed to treat her home as just that. She would rise early, spend time arranging the household to bring it back up to a full complement of servants, interviewing staff and sorting out the supplies needed to keep the place functioning. Eleanor was keen to source as much of the produce needed to supply the Hall as possible from the estate.

Christian had surprised her with the number of questions he asked about the running of the estate. She did not shy away from answering them honestly, suggesting what needed to change or be kept up, continuing the goodwill of the estate workers.

Infrequent rides, lunches and occasionally dinners became more frequent. What had seemed an occasional acquaintance and a mutually beneficial cohabitation was rapidly taking on a more settled routine. It was, she thought, as if they were jointly running the estate, but of course, that could not be, as he owned it and she merely served to bridge gaps in his knowledge and smooth the way between the new owner of the estate and the workers on which he depended.

She had spoken at length with the gardener and Minnie about her plans for the walled garden. She had run her thoughts by Christian first, that they could grow a full range of produce and have preserves, jams, sauces, and dried herbs made for their use and sell on any excess in Northallerton or Thirsk markets. This, with the gardener's and Minnie's knowledge and the added ability of Mrs. Hitchins, who had hesitated to leave, to see how the bottled goods could be made attractive and presented, pleased her. To her delight Christian seemed enthusiastic about her proposals, encouraging ever more of them.

She left the groundsmen and the

tenants to Christian to deal with along with his 'man' who was never far away from his master or the Hall. Even Mrs. Hitchins had stopped complaining about Bill lurking around the place, not being averse to his company at times it seemed. He was the silent figure who solidly served and yet was never referred to by his surname.

In truth, Eleanor was very busy and had so many plans that had culminated from years of frustration of never having her ideas listened to, that she recognised when she was smiling at the garden and planning its future, the feeling of deep satisfaction. So why should she leave? The answer was simple and stark: she would be married off and this home could only ever be a transient one. But at least for now it was hers and so she would enjoy the moments that she could before her future was decided for her. Then she would leave of her own accord, she had corresponded with her friends in Bath. They were open to her visiting.

Christian and Eleanor passed by each

other as they went about their different tasks yet sharing the same world. When they met for a meal, or a drink, Eleanor was pleasantly surprised that her plans were discussed and accepted with little objection or question. He was quite amicable, and she was very aware that he tended to watch her closely. This she took as a sign that he was simply becoming familiar with the notion of being her guardian. In her turn she recognised that she was beginning to seek out opportunities to share time and enjoyed his company. He rarely stayed away and hardly ever visited any clubs that she could ascertain. Christian had never returned inebriated unlike Horace.

'Eleanor!' Christian's voice shouted through the servants' doorway.

'Yes,' she said as she emerged from the stone corridor into the entrance hall.

'Whatever are you doing down there?' He shook his head, raven hair flipped over his white collar, contrasting perfectly, and settling on the finely stitched waistcoat.

He raised his eyebrows at her hesitation. 'I was deciding the menus for next week . . .' Her words drifted off. She had been staring at him, hoping that the pleasant thoughts that had flitted through her mind had not openly shown upon her face. She found him pleasing to the eye and never tired of watching him, unobserved of course.

'Well, have Cook come into the morning room, or Mrs. Hitchins — you should not be down there. Besides, you have spent enough time with the servants. I want you to be seen to have regained your position in the house and join me.' He walked into the withdrawing room.

'Join you?' she repeated following him. 'You want me to visit the tenants with you?'

'Yes, possibly, but let us start by eating together. I wish you to dine with me daily, not occasionally. You shall take your meals when I do when we are both in.' He was facing her, hands on his hips. The daylight behind him showed off his athletic figure. A tall man in long pantaloons and cavalry boots certainly appealed to Eleanor's idea of handsome. It stirred feelings within her that were more exciting than they should be towards her 'guardian', but Christian was no father figure! How would she feel if he began courting some fine lady with a dowry and a well-positioned family? The memory of being the burden upon Jemima and Horace resonated in her mind. Eleanor was thinking of him more and more as belonging to her — like the Hall.

Eleanor was unsure what to say. She had quite got used to the notion of having some of her meals with Minnie and Mrs. Hitchins.

'Very well, do you wish me to dress for dinner?' she asked, her mind whirling as she had got used to the informal nature of daily life, and reverting to the formal version did not appeal to her in the slightest; especially if they were to eat making polite conversation, or in silence.

He laughed as he watched her standing just inside the doorway. 'No, Eleanor,

I do not wish you to dress. I would prefer you to be completely naked. It would make my mealtimes even more entertaining.' He shook his head.

'Your wit surpasses my expectations,' she said quickly, to try and cover her embarrassment and humour at his response, for he was being sarcastic, simply making a quip at her expense, yet the vision of them both being naked together presented a shockingly sinful excitement within her that surprised and delighted.

'I am so glad that you have some expectations of me, Ellie, for I thought you were hiding from me lest I turn into the 'rake' some would still paint me as.' There was a serious note in his voice.

She approached him as she did not want Mrs. Hitchins, or one of the maids, to overhear him using her short name so openly.

'Does it bother you so much about what people think of you? I thought you were above that, Sir Christian, as you dealt with Sir Thomas' comments very well and in a public place.' Eleanor had not been able to completely dismiss the episode from her mind. She looked into his deep sable eyes, wondering what dark and troubled thoughts were making them look duller than normal.

He lifted a finger and stroked her cheek gently. 'Ellie, please call me Christian, I do not want to hear you call me 'sir' like you are one of the servants.'

'Very well, Christian.' She smiled, liking the sound as the name rolled off her tongue and the feel of his brief touch as his hand dropped to his side once more.

'I do not give a fig for what people say about my winning this estate. I care, though, that some are tarnishing you with the stain of living with a 'rake', which is damnably unfair.' He ruffled his hair and stared momentarily at the ceiling.

'It will be my aunt, no doubt, bitter that you have done her out of the allowance she could have had for taking me in,' Eleanor said, and he lowered his chin so they could look into each other's eyes.

'She did that to herself as she turned

you away when you were in need. Shame on her! No, it is more to do with Horace's gambling friends. They are all bad losers, Ellie. They lost their friend who owed them money. I do not owe them so much as a farthing so they will not get anything from me. If they cannot bring me down, then they will try to hurt a softer target — you. One has even offered to take you off my hands for a small dowry that would clear the debt owed him. I hate the man; I think he has even had the cla . . .' He swallowed and shook his head. 'No matter, he will not have you.'

'Who is this man?' she asked.

'No matter, he will not be staking a claim to you and that is the end of it. But they travel amongst the gaming dens and gentlemen's clubs in York, Northallerton and Harrogate and spill their poison into the ears of any who will listen.' He shook his head. 'I should have realised that they would stoop so low.'

'Thank you,' Eleanor said, 'I should have said that to you before now, but you must understand that I had just lost my brother and home. You care about my reputation and safety and that is what a good guardian should do, so I thank you.'

'Had you lost your home, or had it slipped away before my arrival, Ellie?' He folded his arms casually across his body.

'Well, yes, I am only here by your good grace.' She watched a slow smile spread across his face as she had not fully answered his question.

'You were only here as your brother's burden from the minute your mother left this world. Dear Ellie, your home is more yours now than it has ever been.' He placed a hand tenderly on each shoulder and faced her squarely. 'Admit it. I have allowed you to act as the lady of the house, planning, organising dinners and even entertaining my guests, without criticism or making further demands.'

Eleanor was not sure what 'further demands' he was thinking about. 'How so?' she asked. 'There have only been three dinners, Christian. I can cope with that.'

He leaned into her, kissing her forehead ever so gently — sensitively.

She stood there and did not pull away. The sweep of warmth that overcame her senses was not what she had expected. But her heart welcomed it as did her whole body.

Christian looked down at her lips. Before she was even aware he had moved his right hand and cupped her neck gently whilst his mouth found hers and stole away a kiss.

Eleanor gave in to the sweep of sensations emptying her mind of all other thoughts other than the growing intensity of need.

He released her and Eleanor gasped, taking a small step backwards.

Their eyes locked, neither turning away.

'Do I offend you?' he asked.

'No, I mean, yes . . .' She sighed and looked away. 'What is it you want of me, Christian? Do not play games with me for you are a man of this world who has seen war, been with women no doubt, and I have only witnessed personal grief and life at home.'

'Do I scare you?' he asked.

'No . . . but . . . you infuriate me — yes, that is it! You say you want to protect my reputation and yet you behave so boldly . . . so badly.' She shook her head.

'But, Ellie, do you not see that there is a way that this Hall could be your permanent home?'

There was a pause before she responded.

'Are you proposing to me?' she asked — it was a solution that had crossed her mind, but she could not think how to broach it without damaging their newly established friendship. One moment disowned, the next homeless, except for the charity of a servant, then housekeeper, ward and now . . . this! Her world was moving at such a speed. She must keep up or be left behind in the cold.

'No, of course not! I am asking you to be my mistress!' he snapped his words out in too much of a rush.

Eleanor turned to go, but he caught her arm firmly. 'Ellie, my attempt at wit is terrible. Of course, I mean to ask you to marry me. It is just you are beautifully I and wholesome. I only wanted to tease you as you also infuriate me. You run this house like it always should have been. Forgive me for my clumsy approach.' He released her and tried to smile reassuringly.

'You are forgiven, but answer me honestly, Christian, do you love me?' She saw the surprise in his face.

Christian stood away looking at her, bemused. 'Did you not feel excitement when we kissed?'

Eleanor laughed. It was his turn to look instantly taken aback. How easy it would be to destroy his opinion of himself and his ability to conquer her body if not her heart. Yet, if she did, it would be all the worse for her and them. Yes, his touch had ignited her soul and her body longed for it to continue. She wanted to hold his neck to pull him toward her, to feel all of him next to her and yet how shocking these thoughts were.

'You think one stolen kiss would capture my heart? Did you not notice I did not kiss you back, Christian?' she goaded him slightly, not wanting to hurt, but to show him that she was not so easily won over.

'Are you not flattered?' he persisted. She had wrong-footed him and it made Eleanor feel strangely excited that her words had ruffled his normal calm persona so much. She did not smile, for that would be foolish and petty, but the excitement that filled her was replaced by the feeling of joy because he cared deeply about her, and that meant his love for her was surely growing. He may not recognise it yet, but it was there, and she would embrace it, and Christian, heartily but not on the first kiss.

'Yes, of course I am, Christian,' she said softly.

He looked momentarily relieved. 'Then you agree?' he asked.

'I did not say that.' She was going to

say more, but they both heard heavy footsteps approaching the doorway.

Both stood apart as if they had not even been talking to each other.

'Excuse me, sir.' Bill's sturdy form appeared in the doorway.

'Not now, Bill.' Christian was most dismissive.

'Please, carry on,' Eleanor said and began walking to the door. 'We are quite finished.' She walked out without so much as a backwards glance at Christian who stared after her in disbelief.

15

'I could go away, sir,' Bill said in a light-hearted way as Christian glowered at him, annoyed that Eleanor had taken the opportunity to walk away and leave him without her agreement. The little minx! It may not have been the smoothest proposal ever delivered but what did she expect? Theirs was an arrangement of convenience on both sides. He was an excellent catch and she a pretty and useful lady of the house, so why not marry? Then they could have a full relationship and she would come to love him. As for him? Did he love her? Well, yes, but why did she need to ask him when she had been given the role of the lady of the house with his blessing. He had shown trust, respect and given her time to enjoy his company. So, why did she not see he loved her already? He shrugged. What did he know of love, he had been at war for years? Yet her eyes burned with passion — that he recognised — and when he touched her his rose to meet it. He braced himself stopping his imagination from running away with the images that filled his mind. He swallowed and breathed deeply.

'Your timing has never been so abysmal, man.' Christian sighed.

'Really? I thought I normally came to your rescue, sir.' Bill winked.

'Well, this time I did not need rescuing. I was . . .' Christian shook his head. 'I swear I will never understand women.'

Bill came in and found that he was standing by a decanter and glasses. 'Would one of these help?' indicating the decanter with a nod of his head.

'Yes, please. Pour me one. So, what is so urgent that you would choose this moment of my greatest downfall to interrupt?' He sat by the fire and took the offered crystal glass from his friend.

'Is your lady not falling into your carefully thought-out plan, sir?'

Christian laughed ruefully. 'I should have thought it out more carefully. I asked her to marry me, in a manner of speaking.' He swigged back his drink in one and put the glass down on the small table at the side of his chair.

'She refused you! She must be mad!' Bill's voice dripped with sarcasm.

'Not really, but she did not give me a straight answer either. How can she prevaricate? I own this estate, her home. I have wealth and am not unattractive. What does the woman expect? I could match her to a fat oaf who wants a young filly to look after them in their dotage and yet I offer up myself,' he complained.

'Like a lamb to the slaughter,' Bill said, his smile almost breaking into laughter.

'Your point being, man?'

'That perhaps you could humble yourself a little. Appeal to Miss Eleanor's gentler spirit. She may be young. She may be determined to make her home a place that works, but she is still a young lass, and they like to feel wanted . . .'

'I want her, that is obvious!' Christian shook his head. He really had expected her to fly into his arms, all her prayers answered by him.

'Yes, sir, but not just in a carnal way.' Bill winked.

'Next you will be quoting the sonnets. Is this really my hard-headed sergeant speaking or has someone stolen Bill's head?' Christian stared at his friend, knowing that he was the one person in his life who would tell him the God's honest truth in any given situation. He owed the man his life and that was more than enough to share his home with him for as long as he wanted. Bill had nowhere else to go, so the arrangement suited them both well enough.

'Believe Bill when I tell you that a good woman is worth chasing a little. Do not make her feel that she is simply a convenient option who came with the Hall, sir.'

Christian looked at his friend thoughtfully. 'What does Bill know of such tender things?'

'I was young once, sir. I had me a lovely wife, Catherine she was. We had three precious summers together. No babbies, which was just as well really as I would have not been able to look after them, then the war started.' Bill looked down and brushed at invisible threads on his breeches as if in a trance.

'What happened, Bill?'

'She died. The Lord took my beautiful Catherine in a fever that I survived.' He shrugged the past away. 'Life is a bitch at times. So, you like the lass, you take time to make her feel that, wanted, respected. I tell you one month on she will be longing for you to ask her again.' He poured Christian another drink.

'I might change my mind,' Christian said.

'Then you would be a bloody fool, sir, and that you are not.'

'What brings you here? It was not to harangue me on my lack of romantic prowess.'

'Well, we have a game-keeper who should be relocated to the assizes as it seems he has been taking from the tenants, the estate and leading your Mrs. Hitchins a right dance — nice woman that. It's taken a while, but I've sussed out his ways.'

'We shall ride over tomorrow morning and sort him out. You can fill me in on the details over dinner. We'll go to the Hare and Rabbit at Gorebeck, I feel like eating out tonight.'

'Very well, sir, I shall tell Mrs. Hitchins to inform Mrs. Jennings.'

'She should have left by now, shouldn't she?' Christian had quite forgotten that his housekeeper was supposed to have been taking another position.

'Well, sir, you see it was not really a good idea and she is happy here now,' Bill said and smiled as Christian's eyes looked heavenward.

'Oh well, as long as she is happy. So, tell me then, when was she going to ask me if she could stay and revoke her hastily tendered and accepted resignation?' His tone was very sarcastic as he stared at Bill who was still smiling back at him.

'No need, sir, Miss Eleanor told her it was advisable for her to stay on.

'Bill, she is a block of ice, I do not need

to see her drifting around the shadows of my home,' Christian said.

'Ah, you are too harsh by half. Gertrude is a gentle soul and you scared her. Give her a chance too.'

'Good grief, you and 'Gertrude' are friends! You cannot be serious, you and the ice-maiden?' Christian ran his hand through his hair. 'These women are infuriating to me. Ellie did not jump at the chance of becoming my wife. I told her the Hall could be her home again. I have a good mind to send her to a convent to think it through. Then she might look kindlier upon my offer.' Christian placed his glass down firmly.

'That would be unwise, sir. She has an eye for you, but you need to ingratiate yourself. The lass has had shock on shock, and you come in and take over the place and expect her to be grateful within a few weeks. She is spreading her wings and learning to fly, give her time before you clip them.'

'Fetch the horse, Bill, we will ride into Gorebeck. I think you need some fresh air. I know I do.'

Christian stormed out, whilst Bill more steadily stood and shook his head ruefully.

* * *

'Well, what did you find out about Squires?' Christian finally asked Bill once they were established in a corner settle in the Hare and Rabbit.

'It appears he has been causing trouble with the tenants. Scaring them into paying more, in kind if not in rent, threatening them with eviction, claiming to have the new master's ear and warning them against speaking out.'

'Damn!' Christian shook his head. He had given the man the rope with which to hang himself. Wanting to know who he could trust and who not. Christian, via Bill, had given people on his estate tasks to do, the responsibility for their part of the working of the estate, to see who came through with good and honest hard work which would show its own reward through their resulting goods or crops, provided they were honest and would reveal who abused the opportunity and his trust.

Samuel had proved to be a good and honest man at the dairy farm. Hitchins had been a pain to Christian, dour natured whenever he was around, but Eleanor had praised her immaculate records and housekeeping abilities. Cook was frugal, but always provided edible fayre, the stable hands had spent wisely on improving the stables, the gardeners had only put some aside for the odd nip of brandy to fend off the cold in adverse weather, but the man who had proven himself to be a cheat, bully and a liar was the gamekeeper. It had taken Bill a few weeks to gain trust and unearth the truth of what had been going on in the background. Now he told Christian the detail of what he had discovered. Whilst the man presented a working estate, subject to sheep rustling and poor crops through lazy tenants. He had actually been selling off small numbers of sheep regularly and taking part of the farmers' profits to line his own pockets.

'Do you know when he next plans to round some sheep up and with whom?' Christian asked, keeping his voice low, well below the noise and banter inside the place.

'No, not precisely, but I have been following him these last few days and he was seen with Jason Mannish three times.'

'Bell Cottage tenant?' Christian remembered the man. Built like a house end. His tenancy was not the best kept and yet he looked like he had enough to fill his fat belly.

'Aye, sir, Squires has been emptying Mannish's sheep pen again. Just took six of his sheep to market, sold the wool and the meat, so no intention of keeping the animals for more wool. That is how he does it, a few at a time.'

'We'll need to borrow a few of the Yeomanry, Bill. I want him caught, removed, and punished. I do not want anyone else pointing fingers in my direction and swearing I am removing innocent men who served the estate for a long time.'

'Then we should visit their captain in the morning, and I'll tip him the wink when the sheep pen is refilled. Meanwhile, you must come up with your own plan of action . . .'

'Crawled out from under your stone, I see, Low-Bolton!' The slightly slurred voice derided his name as he shouted over to Christian across the tap room.

Sir Thomas Ellerby had just appeared at the bottom of the wooden stairwell.

'Ellerby, whose bed have you just crawled out from, not your wife's, I presume,' Christian replied in a lighthearted voice and was pleased that there was a ripple of laughter throughout the room.

'You blackguard, we are not all made of your low morals,' Sir Thomas blustered as he strode over to Christian's table. Bill had his back to the man who was focused on Christian alone. When Sir Thomas saw Christian's ex sergeant look up at him, he did not step any closer.

Four other gentlemen descended the stairs joking, their banter only ceasing once they saw their friend standing staring at Christian. Obviously to him these men had just alighted from a closed game and by the expression on Sir Thomas Ellerby's face he had not fared well.

'Come, Ellerby, he is not worth your breath. Leave him.' Charles Dewsbury swept an arm around Sir Thomas and the man allowed himself to be turned away professing how Charles had prevented him from calling Christian out but going willingly enough.

'You know, sir, if I could find some dirt to dish on that bastard I would happily do so,' Bill said watching Sir Thomas' back.

'I know, Bill, but he has friends who have friends so to make anything stick fast to him, it would have to be good. It would have to go beyond the local magistrate, one Charles Dewsbury, and to an independent authority who could usurp their band of rogues.'

Bill sat back and grinned. 'Hmm, that's what I thought. It would have to be justice which was not meted out by the local magistrate.'

'Bill, stand down, man. I have enough on my plate at the moment. I do not want to have to dig you out of a deep dark cell somewhere because of a rash act. That man will go the way of Horace. He has debts already.'

'You know this for certain?' Bill asked.

'Yes, for very soon I will call them in.' He looked at Bill and winked.

'Well, I'll drink to that,' he said and downed the rest of his tankard.

16

Christian and Bill prepared to leave the inn to ride back to the estate. The dark of night had engulfed the inn. Bill went to collect their horses, he was not a man to be taken off guard easily, but when a club hit him from behind as he entered the stables he fell like a bull on ice.

Christian waited outside the inn for a few moments but when all was quiet, and no horses emerged led by Bill, his senses piqued — something was wrong. The natural thing to do would be to go around the to the stable and shout for his friend, but he had been in an army where he had entered enemy villages with his men, watching for snipers lurking in the shadows or on roof tops, ready to ambush them. There was always an unusual stillness to the places when the threat of death lurked. His sixth sense was telling him all was far from well in this sleepy northern market town.

Christian slipped back inside the inn, walking past the serving hatch and beyond the tap room. Only a few heads turned. He stopped in the short corridor before the back door, where he loaded his pistol.

Slipping outside again into the cold night air he kept his pistol to his side and crossed the cobblestones as stealthily as he could, entering the stables with caution. A horse was tethered at the back of the inn, but it was not one of theirs. When the club swung at him, he ducked, catching a blow to his shoulder that stunned his firing arm for a second. Bill stood unsteadily and their attacker fled, jumping atop his waiting horse. Christian aimed and shot, the man yelped as he disappeared around the corner of the inn and galloped off down the open road that would lead up to Gorebeck moor, disappearing into the night.

'You alright, sir?' Bill asked groggily, still not managing to stand up straight. Blood stained the back of his head and jacket. Christian had been about to mount his horse and follow their attacker when his friend sank heavily to the floor. Instantly Christian was at his side. Bill had fought in battles and never fallen; how could he be felled so easily in a Yorkshire market town at peace — why? Christian looked up at the approaching figures.

The shot had alerted the innkeeper who arrived with a couple of his men from the inn.

'What the hell happened here . . . sir?' he added the title as he got a better look at Christian.

'Did you see who it was?' Christian asked, as he stood straight.

Blank faces stared back at him, not comprehending what had happened, any more than Christian had.

'Damnation! Two of you mount up and seek the coward out. He headed up the moor road. The others get this man inside quickly and carefully! Have him carried to your best room and summon Doctor Speers. If he is in his bed insist that I will see to his inconvenience but get him here as soon as possible. This man is injured. Treat him well, he fought at Waterloo and is a hero this country owes much to.' Christian snapped out his orders and then turned his attention to going to his horse that was saddled in the end stall. He felt a wave of emotion sweep through him, which bordered on fear. He had not experienced such since they were at war, but then his trusty sergeant had always been there to make a joke, take the edge of the death and drama, and watch his back. Now he felt exposed and filled with a strong desire to lash out at whoever did this.

'Yes, sir,' the innkeeper replied, and turned to the men, repeating Christian's instructions. 'You heard him, at once!' Two men rode out at speed in the direction of the attacker and the rest carried a mumbling Bill into the inn.

His incomprehensible mutterings and curses gave solace to Christian's ears. The man was tough, he would be fine.

Christian walked down to his horse; perhaps he could catch them up, but his heart wanted to stay and make sure his friend was alright. Bill had scouted, found him, and carried him back to camp. 'Damnation!' he cursed. He owed the man a good retirement, a long life, a chance to be happy again.

He stepped into the stall and aimed his pistol as movement at the back caught his eye, whoever was there would not know he had not reloaded, but he lowered it when he realised it was no more than a frightened stable lad hiding in the corner who, thinking his life might be about to end curled tightly into a foetal position. Petrified eyes stared back at him.

Like a cornered cat he suddenly sprang up and tried to use an upturned pail to jump up and over the partition and into the next stall in a futile attempt to escape.

Christian caught him with his free hand and pushed his slight frame against the side of the stall, taking the wind from his lungs and pinning him there by the scruff of his neck with one hand. The other pushed the barrel of the pistol to the lad's side. His body slumped as he slid back down until his feet supported his weight on the floor.

The men in the inn may not have seen who the man was, but Christian realised he had just found a witness, he would protect the lad but find out who had tried to injure or kill them. Unless the lad refused to talk freely about what happened, then he would throw him into gaol and make sure he did not see light of day until he spoke.

'Who was it?' Christian shouted at his frightened face, watching him flinch.

The lad tried to shake his head.

Christian released his grip and stood back, but the pistol was trained on him; he was going nowhere.

'I will ask once more and you will tell me the God's honest truth, or you will go down in chains into the lock-up and, believe me, I will hold the key to your release and no one else,' Christian promised, not shouting but speaking plainly. 'Tell me now!'

The lad shook his head at his words.

Christian realised that for him to refuse meant that whoever had lain in wait for them must have a strong influence, frightening the lad out of his wits and senses, for he was scared stiff and had a gun pointed at him.

'He'll kill me . . . I didn't see nought . . .' He swallowed and tried to bravely put his chin up. Tears fell from the corner of his eyes.

Christian would have felt pity for him if it was not for the blood that had stained his own hand from the back of his sergeant's head.

The lad was just about old enough to be a drummer boy. Cannon fodder. But he would not need to be that anymore. Bill and Christian and those who had fought for most of their adult lives had seen to that for him. But Christian was in no mood to be lenient to a frightened pup that held the name of a man who had tried to take them down.

'They'll come out of the inn. They'll not let a stranger hurt me,' the lad said as he sniffled.

Christian realised he had a good point. With one hand he grabbed the boy by his collar and dragged him over the back of his horse. He jumped up and rode for ten minutes beyond the village and into the woodland. There he pushed the lad to the floor, jumped down and placed the barrel of the, still unloaded, gun to the lad's head.

'Now there is no one but you and me.' Christian cocked the gun. He felt him shake. His experience within the regiment gave him the confidence to push the lad into speaking the truth. Christian wanted him to say it was Sir Thomas Ellerby and he would have the man, even if he had to go to the next county to get a decent magistrate to bring him down.

'It was John Squires!' The lad held his head in his hands.

Christian stepped away and got back on the horse, flinching at the effort it took on his bruised shoulder. He was shaken. He had known the man was a sheep rustler and had creamed money off his tenants, but to attack them — try to kill them in cold blood — that took an evil mind. His own tenant! Christian had returned here wanting to find a home, peace, and a new start; had found Ellie; every cloud had a silver lining, Bill would say. Ellie was pure gold. But Squires was going to see justice done. Now he knew who the coward was he would check on Bill, for he knew that Squires was going nowhere fast. If he thought he had got away with it, he would carry on his life as normal.

'You're not going to shoot me?' the lad asked as he got to his feet, looking at Christian with relief.

'Never was,' Christian said as he held an arm out for the lad to climb up on the horse behind him. 'I don't shoot boys. But you cannot stand by and watch an attack upon an innocent man and not do or say something — unless you are a coward.'

The lad wiped his eyes with the back of his sleeve.

'He will, he'll wait, and he'll beat me to a pulp and leave me in the bog up on the moor. He told me so and I believe him for that was how Ned disappeared and he . . .' The lad looked away; lips clenched shut as if he had already said too much.

'Who was Ned?' Christian wondered if the man was already a murderer as well as a thief.

'His dog, it went deaf, but it was still a good dog . . .' The lad was struggling not to blubber.

Christian felt a flood of relief, but he could see the pain in the lad's face.

'Do you want a ride home?' Christian asked.

He shook his head. 'No, it wouldn't do to be seen with you. I'll walk back from here.'

'Where is home, lad?' Christian asked.

'Bell Cottage,' he said.

'You're a Mannish?' Christian asked, realising that the lad's father was about to be arrested for sheep rustling too.

He nodded.

'Well, our paths will cross again, and soon.' Christian held the reins firmly.

What a mess this was turning into.

'Squires threatened Pa with eviction, you know. I have four sisters and a sickly ma,' the lad said before Christian turned the horse to return to the road again.

'Does he profit from the estate's losses?' Christian asked. 'Your pa?'

The lad shook his head. 'Only by keeping the cottage in good order, the land fertile and his sheep pen open for Squires' use.'

'What is your name?' Christian asked, realising the boy was trying to clear his father from any willing involvement with Squires' actions.

'Dan, sir.' He said and approached the side of the horse.

'Then say nothing, Dan. Not to your pa or anyone. You were not there; you saw nothing and never spoke to me. If your father is a good man then I will not see harm done to him, or your family, but Squires will fall.'

The lad nodded and Christian returned to Gorebeck and to Bill. He arrived as Doctor Speers did; they walked into the room where Bill slept; it was eerily quiet.

* * *

'Miss Eleanor,' the troubled voice of Mrs. Hitchins burst into the morning room as Eleanor finished her breakfast, alone. Christian had not appeared. His place setting lay undisturbed.

'Whatever is it Mrs. Hitchins, you look quite pale?' Eleanor stood up and met the woman as she entered the room.

'Minerva has just told me, that the dairy man told her, that they were attacked last night.' The woman was clearly babbling as she was in shock.

Eleanor looked at her. 'Calmly now, Mrs. Hitchins. Who would attack the dairy farmers — or do you mean the cows?' Eleanor's mind was in a spin. Where on earth was Christian? If there was trouble of this nature on the estate, then she needed him there. Disputes she could sort out, but violence of any kind needed Christian, Squires or Bill's presence.

'No, Miss Eleanor, Sir Christian and Bill, they were attacked and are still in the town . . . Doctor Speers was sent for.'

'Goodness! Are they badly hurt? We must go to them and see. Has the doctor been in attendance for both of them?' Eleanor was rushing out of the room. 'Annie, Florrie, one of you fetch my pelisse and get word to Squires, we need the carriage. He will have to come and take us.'

Mrs. Hitchins hesitated before leaving. 'Yes, we shall both go, Miss Eleanor. I think he was just there to see Bill. He is tough, he will be fine, won't he?'

What on earth was she fussing about Bill for when Christian could have been struck down and in goodness knows what condition. 'Of course,' Eleanor snapped, 'now send young Jeremiah to find Squires urgently, we need the carriage now!'

'Yes, yes straight away.' Mrs. Hitchins scurried down to the kitchen. Eleanor quickly dressed for the journey, hoping, and praying that Christian was alright.

Bill was as tough as old nails, but Christian was a gentleman — her gentleman. He was brave but not so hardy. She stepped outside the Hall and waited as she saw Jeremiah riding back towards the house with Squires.

'Miss Eleanor, do you know what happened, ma'am?' Squires said as he rode up in front of her. The four steps leading to the Hall's entrance placed her above his head height. The man was rugged, dressed in a coat of good hardy cloth with a robust broad brimmed hat that shielded his eyes from the autumnal sun and from her.

'No, Squires. Please hurry things along. Mrs. Hitchins and I need to find out what has occurred. All I know is that they were attacked in Gorebeck and now are at the Hare and Rabbit. We must make haste!'

'Yes, miss, of course.' He kicked the horse so that it cantered around into the yard.

'Thank goodness,' Eleanor said. For in the absence of Christian and Bill, at least she had a loyal servant to take her to town. Squires knew the estate and neighbouring ones well as he had been born on one of them — she forgot which one. He had come to work for Horace when their father died and knew everyone in the region. Her mother's failing health had placed an extra burden upon Horace's shoulders which he had shared with this man in running the estate. So, he would know what to do about summoning Charles Dewsbury, the local magistrate, if it had not been done already. Why they should have been attacked, puzzled Eleanor. It was not like they were connected with the milling industry that had caused such uproar in other parts of the county and beyond. What was the world coming to? This was supposed to be a time of peace — war had ended. Yet there was so much uncertainty and unrest in the country.

Once the coach appeared, Mrs. Hitchins stepped outside the Hall, with Minnie ready to wave them off.

Squires pulled on the brake and stepped down gingerly from the front plate. He smiled quickly as he saw Eleanor's look of concern. 'Just a stitch in my side miss, I came over here a bit quick like when I heard the news.' He opened the carriage door for them.

'You don't need to worry none. Sir Christian and Bill are soldiers, Eleanor, they'll be fine,' Minnie shouted down to them from the Hall's doorway. 'Take good care of them, John,' she added.

'Of course, Mrs. Jennings, or my name's not John Squires!' he said and winked up at the cook as Eleanor and Mrs. Hitchins took their seats inside.

The coach lurched forward. Eleanor was surprised at how distraught Mrs. Hitchins was.

'You really care for Bill that much?' she asked, amazed that whilst she had been growing in affection for Christian her housekeeper had become attached to his friend. It was the only explanation why her housekeeper would be so shaken up by the thought of Bill being hurt. Her own panic at the thought of Christian being taken from her and how much she cared for him threatened to spill over also. She swallowed and took hold of Mrs. Hitchins' hand. 'Oh, what a pair we are, and we have no idea if they are badly hurt or not. We must be strong, Gertrude!'

The woman smiled at Eleanor's use of her Christian name. 'Bill has not yet woken up since he was struck on the back of the head, Miss Eleanor. I found that bit out from the stable lad who had met someone from town when he was out exercising one of the animals early this morning.'

'Oh dear. But with a good restorative sleep he should be fine. What of Christian?' Eleanor asked and braced herself lest she knew something equally worrying about him.

'He was not hurt. Sir Christian has stayed with Bill. Oh, how worried about Bill he must be! Why, Miss Eleanor, is it that happiness has been waved in my path once more only to be beaten away by fate again?' The woman sniffed.

Eleanor let go of her hand. 'He is not dead, Mrs. Hitchins, compose yourself, please. I will see he has the absolute best of care.' Eleanor did not mean to sound harsh, but she could not have the woman crumble in the coach. They needed to be strong and have clear heads.

'Yes, yes of course, forgive me. I speak out of turn . . .' Mrs. Hitchins voice broke.

'No, Gertrude, forgive my harsh words for you speak out of love. Something we all need and sometimes have without even realising it until the threat of its removal is made.'

Eleanor blinked away tears.

'Then perhaps we shall both have our chance of happiness restored,' Mrs. Hitchins said and smiled a genuinely sweet smile.

How lonely a life Mrs. Hitchins has had, Eleanor thought. She promised herself in that moment that if God permitted Bill to live, and Christian to forgive her highhandedness when he offered to marry her, that she would accept him at the first opportunity she had and see that Mrs. Hitchins and Bill also had that same opportunity if they wished it.

But who would do such a thing? Sir Thomas Ellerby hated Christian, but he was no street brawler, but something niggled at the back of her mind. She needed to see Christian and find out what happened before blaming innocent parties.

They crossed the old bridge by the Norman church and turned towards the Hare and Rabbit. Very soon she would have her answers, and all would be well.

17

The coach pulled up alongside the inn. Mrs. Hitchins was so keen to go inside that she opened the door before the brake was applied fully and nearly slipped off the seat.

'Gertrude!' Eleanor shook her head; the woman was like a love-sick child.

'Sorry,' Mrs. Hitchins said and sat back on the cushion, her hands gripping each other on her lap.

Squires appeared at the door and opened it for them. 'Let me find the stable lad and then I'll go in and ask what the situation is, miss,' he said, and looked surprised when Eleanor stepped out of the carriage, shortly followed by Mrs. Hitchins.

'You stay with the coach, Squires. We shall go in and ask for the stable lad to be sent around to you and then you can enter. I have no wish to be left in an unattended coach.' She walked towards the door, noticing that, although Squires nodded, he looked far from pleased.

Eleanor took a moment for her eyes to adjust to the dim light within the inn. She avoided the tap room and headed for the newly created reception area that led to the modern dining room and the newer part of the hotel.

'Can I help you, miss?' a soldier in the smart uniform of the local Yeomanry asked. Unlike the soldiers who had returned in battered and patched together worn outfits, the local Yeomanry had a fine livery of blue and grey with white brocade on their officers' jackets. He carried his shako under his arm with pride.

'Yes, please. We are looking for Sir Christian Leigh-Bolton and his man, Bill.' Eleanor realised that she had never known or used Bill's surname. How strange things had been since Horace and Jemima parted. Lines were being blurred and yet she no longer cared.

'Ah, yes, I too have been sent to see them.' He looked at Mrs. Hitchins who quickly stepped forward.

'Are they well? Will they live?' she asked, and Eleanor cast her an amazed glance. The woman would have a faint if she kept this up.

'Yes, Mrs. . . .'

'Mrs. Hitchins,' she added.

'Yes, Mrs. Hitchins, they are both alive. Doctor Speers informed me that Captain Leigh-Bolton has a bruised shoulder, but is fine, and his ex-sergeant breathes more evenly, but will have one nasty headache when he regains consciousness.' He smiled reassuringly back at them. 'Please come with me. I shall take you to Captain Leigh-Bolton and he can answer your questions directly. You are Miss Richards, I take it?' he addressed Eleanor.

'Yes,' she said as she followed him up a flight of stairs to a recently carpeted corridor.

'Then you have saved my man a journey to Kinsley Hall for we were asked to convey a message to you that all would be well.' He stopped at a door. 'If you would wait here a moment I will ask if it is suitable for ladies to enter, or if Captain Leigh-Bolton will see you downstairs in the lounge area. Forgive me if I have brought you up here for no reason.'

'You are forgiven,' Eleanor said.

The man slipped inside the room.

'Well!' Mrs. Hitchins said, 'Who does he think he is?'

'The captain of the local Yeomanry!' Eleanor said quietly, 'And you are a housekeeper and a lady so it is right that we should not burst into a man's bedchamber in an inn, isn't it?'

'I suppose so, but Bill could be . . .'

'Gertrude!' Eleanor snapped and the woman started but nodded and composed herself again.

She might wait outside but Eleanor eagerly listened with her ear to the door.

'Captain, I am so glad you have arrived,' Christian was saying.

'I am not the only one, sir. Miss Richards and her woman have arrived, seemingly very concerned for the safety of you both.'

‘Really! Wonderful! That will save you some time and guarantees they are kept safe. I will see them in a moment. I need you to take men and arrest my groundsman, John Squires. He attacked us last night.’ Christian coughed.

‘You have proof that it was this man? You saw him?’ The captain looked doubtfully down at a very disorientated Bill on the bed who had clearly been hit from behind.

‘No, not a witness as such, but you get the man and you will see he has an injury to his side where I winged him with a bullet from my pistol,’ Christian explained.

‘Where will I find this man? How do you know he has not gone to ground already?’ the captain said, and then added, ‘No pun intended, sir.’

‘This is no laughing matter. I do not know, but you will have to find him before he does.’

‘He is here!’ Eleanor burst in. She cared not if they knew she had eavesdropped. This all made sense now. The man did not have a stitch in his side, he had a wound. 'He brought us in the coach, Christian.'

'Then we have him!' Christian said, but as they spoke a horse was heard galloping away from outside the inn. Turning rapidly to the window Christian saw Dan staggering out of the stable, holding the side of his face.

'Damn him!' Christian cursed.

'We'll find him, don't worry, sir,' the captain said and left the room in great haste. Mrs. Hitchins went straight to Bill's side. The man looked up and half smiled, grimaced at the effort of moving his head and closed his eyes again.

'Mrs. Hitchins, would you stay and see he is kept safe?' Christian asked.

'Of course,' she said and pulled over a chair to sit by the man's bedside.

Christian walked over to Eleanor and cupping her elbow, stepped outside the room. In the privacy of the corridor, he kissed her tenderly on her welcoming lips, but then stood straight.

'Christian, I was so worried for you.'

She lifted on tiptoe and returned the kiss.

He flinched as her hand pressed on his shoulder to raise herself higher. Instantly she stepped back.

'It's only a bruise,' he said dismissively.

'Will Bill be alright?' she asked.

'Yes, but for a few hours I was frightened I had lost him, Ellie. That on top of the thought of losing you too, for you are so against accepting my proposal. I thought we could have a loving future together as man and wife. You may not love me now, but in marriages that are arranged this can grow afterwards — can't it?' He cast his eyes down as if ashamed of his entreaty.

'I never said that I did not love you. Neither did I reject you. That I will never do, Christian. I was just too proud and blind to admit it. Fate has brought us together and . . .' she fell silent.

'What is it?' Christian saw a look of realisation dawn upon her face as she stopped speaking.

'Christian, I believe Sir Thomas

Ellerby is behind this attack. He hates you, despises me for not taking up with his friend's offer, and living under your roof. He is also owed money by Horace or was.' Eleanor was quite certain she had sorted out the problem.

'I thought so too, but it was definitely Squires who attacked us and there is no connection between them that I know of.' He stroked her cheek gently with his hand and she leaned into it.

'Yes, there is. You see Squires was raised on his estate. He was sent over here to help Horace run the tenancies, for he had no notion how the estate worked, and Thomas offered Squires as a good man of excellent character and knowledge. He seemed so efficient, and Horace trusted him.'

'Then if the man goes to ground now, in panic, he will return to his master. You must stay here with Mrs. Hitchins, and I will sort this mess out with the captain. They will be looking on the wrong estate.'

'No . . . I . . .'

'Yes, because if Bill awakes properly, it will take the two of you to hold him down and prevent him trying to come after me . . . Promise?' He was holding both of her shoulders and looking straight into her worried eyes.

'Very well, Christian. But stay safe.'

He kissed her full on her mouth, lingering a delicious moment, which was only cut short when voices were heard on the stairs. He pulled away, opened the bedchamber door, and bustled her inside, closing it quickly before they could be seen together.

* * *

Eleanor arranged for broth to be sent to Bill's room for the three of them, although she sat by the window overlooking the street waiting for any sign of a return by Christian.

Mrs. Hitchins spooned delicate mouthfuls of the warming liquid into Bill's mouth after the two of them managed to prop him up on a bolster pillow.

His colour, initially drained, gradually came back as did a slightly tremulous smile.

Once his wits seemed to return fully, Eleanor could see the light of love flicker in his eyes as it mirrored Mrs. Hitchins. She felt a little awkward and was tempted to leave them alone, but in an inn, even a respectable one, on her own, she dared not.

It was hours later that Christian finally returned to her. The door opened and the cold air wafted into the room.

'Thought you'd abandoned me in heaven,' Bill quipped as he glanced from one woman to the other.

'Good to see you looking chipper, Bill. How's the head?' Christian asked as he walked over to Eleanor who was seated by the window.

'It's been better, but I am a hard nut to crack. Did you find the b . . . blighter?' Bill asked, his eyes fixed on Christian's face.

'Squires is now in the lock up. We took him all the way down to York — save the local magistrate from the hassle of judging him.' He winked knowing Squires had friends who would help him escape given half a chance if he was kept in Gorebeck. 'I have set all the charges and he will languish there until the next assizes.'

Bill half smiled his approval. He obviously could not shake his head or nod.

'Did you have Sir Thomas arrested too?' Eleanor asked, looking up into Christian's tired eyes.

'No proof would stick to him to remove the dirt that encases his good name. We only have the accusations of a liar and a thief — Squires — if he admitted it. Chances are he would rely on Thomas and his friends to find a way of getting him out.' Christian shrugged and sat down next to Eleanor, holding her hand in his.

'Then he walks away and can try to hurt you again,' she said.

'No, that he will not. For, you see, he has been summoned to pay a debt of £2,578 3s 7d by tomorrow night, which he cannot pay. So, he will be escorted to debtors' prison tomorrow and his wife to her sisters in Hastings. I have arranged transport for her. The estate will be sold.' Christian smiled. 'I own the man's debts, you see. I made sure I acquired them when I realised he was out to make trouble. He may be able to evade the law on many things, protected by privilege and his magistrate friend Charles Dewsbury, but a called in debt — or in his case debts — cannot be escaped so easily.'

Eleanor hugged him and Bill raised his eyebrows at Mrs. Hitchins who surprised him by kissing his cheek ever so quickly as he squeezed her hand.

'When can we go home?' Bill asked.

Christian smiled. 'We all return to Kinsley Hall this night. Come, Eleanor, we shall have the coach made ready. It is time our family was settled into the Hall. Bill, I have a need for a good estate manager and groundsman. It is a position that comes with a soon to be built cottage on the estate. You are welcome to live in Kinsley until then, where Mrs.

Hitchins can oversee your full recovery.'

The woman blushed.

Bill chuckled. 'Sounds good to me,' he said.

'Come down when you are both ready. We will be in the lounge.'

* * *

Before they left the landing, Christian swept Eleanor into his arms. Eyes flared with passion, the air between them was charged. 'Now, answer me, woman, without interruption.' He fell to his knee still holding her hands. 'Will you be my wife?'

Eleanor's hand cupped the nape of his neck, her fingers rippled through the tendrils of his hair. His hand slipped around her waist as he pulled her to him.

Eleanor slid down to kneel too, her lips met his, urgent and tender. Christian moaned deep within his throat. They melted into each other; their arms encircled. The softness of her cheek rested against the fine weave of his coat.

'Yes!' she said resting in his embrace as if they would never part but did when a startled captain appeared at the top of the staircase. He coughed and both stood, holding hands, and laughing.

'Be the first to congratulate me, captain! We are to wed,' Eleanor said, and the man shook Christian's hand in congratulation before Christian and Eleanor stepped out into the world together — her heart and home secure.

Ulverscroft Large Print Books Ltd.,
The Green, Bradgate Road, Anstey,
Leicester, LE7 7FU, England.
Tel: (00 44) **0116 236 4325**
Fax: (00 44) **0116 234 0205**

Other titles in the Linford Romance Library:

LIGHTS, CAMERA, ACTION!

Wendy Janes

Along with five other couples, cash-strapped Hayley and Craig are flown to a romantic island paradise as contestants in a new upmarket TV programme: Britain's Most Romantic Couple. There's a £100,000 prize up for grabs for the winners.

Relationships are put under the spotlight, and friendships and rivalries emerge, as the couples attempt entertaining creative, physical and practical tasks.

Will Hayley and Craig show they deserve to be crowned Britain's Most Romantic Couple?

A RISK WORTH TAKING

Alyson Hilbourne

Meg and her father run a public house by the sea, but Pa is also involved in the 'night business' — helping the smugglers evade the excise men. More than anything, Meg wishes he could get out of the gang's clutches; but when Pa brings home an injured man to hide in their attic, it seems the family will be more involved than ever . . .

NUMBER ONE FAN

Debbie Chase

Ordinary Yorkshire girl Angie-Marie gets the break of a lifetime and becomes international pop sensation Anya Starr. But the path to stardom is never a smooth one, and Anya soon realises that not everyone is what they seem . . .